She could feel the heat rising again, and she didn't even bother with the excuse of hormones

Sarah knew better.

It was all Hunt. She liked him. More than liked him. She hadn't come looking for it, and she'd certainly tried to avoid it. But no matter what, she couldn't kid herself any longer.

Maybe she was attracted to him because it proved that she was still a desirable woman. And maybe he was attracted to her because it proved an inner potency, a life force that had been restored.

If it was mutually self-serving, so be it. But it was also no use pretending any longer that something wasn't happening between them. And that something was inevitable, as well.

So what did she say after such a revelation?

"Gee, that was a novel way to wrap up a prenatal visit" was the best she could come up with.

"You think that wraps things up?" he asked.

"You and I both 'replied with a

Dear Reader,

Welcome back to Grantham and back to school! Ever since writing *Falling for the Teacher*, I have wanted to tell Sarah and Hunt's story. Sarah intrigued me because on the surface she looked like someone in control. But I had a feeling there was more lurking underneath. What I found was a woman like many of us, someone who has made choices in life, but still wasn't sure where she was going. In short, she was in search of her story. By contrast, Hunt was someone who had his life all figured out, only to find it pulled out from under him. He realized he needed to change direction, but to where and for how long? In essence, he questioned his future. Together, then, Sarah and Hunt were just too good to leave in the background!

Lastly, cancer has an insidious way of touching many families. This book deals with the impact of lymphoma. For those readers seeking more information about blood cancers, the Leukemia and Lymphoma Society provides helpful and unbiased information at www.leukemia-lymphoma.org.

Best,

Tracy Kelleher

Family Be Mine
Tracy Kelleher

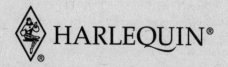

TORONTO • NEW YORK • LONDON
AMSTERDAM • PARIS • SYDNEY • HAMBURG
STOCKHOLM • ATHENS • TOKYO • MILAN • MADRID
PRAGUE • WARSAW • BUDAPEST • AUCKLAND

Recycling programs
for this product may
not exist in your area.

ISBN-13: 978-0-373-71678-4

FAMILY BE MINE

Copyright © 2010 by Louise Handelman

ABOUT THE AUTHOR

Tracy sold her first story to a children's magazine when she was ten years old. Writing was clearly in her blood, though fiction was put on hold while she received degrees from Yale and Cornell, traveled the world, worked in advertising, became a staff reporter and later a magazine editor. She also managed to raise a family. Is it any surprise she escapes to the world of fiction?

Books by Tracy Kelleher

HARLEQUIN SUPERROMANCE

Don't miss any of our special offers. Write to us at the following address for information on our newest releases.

Harlequin Reader Service
U.S.: 3010 Walden Ave., P.O. Box 1325, Buffalo, NY 14269
Canadian: P.O. Box 609, Fort Erie, Ont. L2A 5X3

Many thanks to Dr. Morton Coleman
for sharing his expertise and understanding.

CHAPTER ONE

May...

"YOU KNOW, SARAH DEAR, today's blessed event makes up for that whole Brooklyn calamity..." Penny Halverson bit her bottom lip. "No, I promised I wouldn't bring that up. What I mean to say is that you having a wedding in the Grantham University Chapel is...is...like a dream come true. To think that a member of our family is about to be married in a place like that! It's practically like being in England! Or Disney World!"

Penny dabbed the corner of her eye with the all-cotton hanky that she had ironed just before packing her suitcase for the flight from Minneapolis to Grantham, New Jersey. Even within the confines of the church vestry, the mullioned windows and ornate woodwork conveyed the Gothic grandeur of the Ivy League university chapel. But the fact that Penny's face shone with a rosy hue had nothing to do with the light piercing the stained glass windows. It was the glow of a mother's joy—and maybe unexpected heat of this early May day.

Outside, visible through an open door, were beds of Rembrandt tulips edging the green of the courtyard. Their variegated petals flopped in exhaustion. They had managed to survive the ravenous appetite of the local deer population, perhaps a show of respect by the animal kingdom for this hallowed spot, but they were now succumbing to the heat.

"Oh, I know I promised, but I can't help it." Penny pursed her lips and squinted her eyes in a mixture of remorse and pride. "It more than makes up for the embarrassment that your father felt when you…ah…when you…ah."

"When I was living with Earl? Is that what you're trying to say, Mom?" Sarah Halverson rolled her shoulders backward and worked at adjusting the neckline on her strapless wedding dress. The fitted bodice tapered to hug her long torso a tad too tightly for comfort. "I know you and Dad didn't approve, and I'm sorry. But, you know, it's really not a crime," she said as she yanked at the stays under her arms and hunched her shoulders together to try to get all the pieces to work in harmony. "Practically everybody I know is doing it or has done it at one time."

Actually, that wasn't true. Take her two best friends. Katarina had come back to Grantham to recuperate from a terrible shooting, found the love of her life, and was now happily married to financial wizard Ben Brown. Ben pretended to be cantankerous but was really a pussycat, a pussycat with a teenage son. Besides acquiring a family, Katarina had also started a new business of advising retirees on total financial and lifestyle planning.

And her other best friend Julie was a dedicated obstetrician, *way* too busy to form any lasting relationship—or so she claimed. More likely, she was too tall for most men and too…well…frank. "I'm not brutal, merely blunt," Julie would protest over her third Rolling Rock. Julie pooh-poohed high-priced beers, describing microbrews as "fancy labels for dilettante, candy-assed drinkers."

Sarah, who cherished Julie more than most, found that proclamation more than blunt. After all, her fiancé and very-soon-to-be husband, Zach, thought of himself as something of an expert on high-end beers. He regularly lectured Sarah on the pros and cons of various Belgium brews. "I'm just trying to expand your horizons," he was fond of saying after a typical fifteen-minute discourse.

Not that Sarah minded. Because while she might chide her mother about her parochial concerns, the truth of the matter was, Earl had been a deadbeat. Back in her callow youth, Sarah had thought Earl was a rebel who had needed to burst the bonds of rural Minnesota to pursue a rock music career. But Earl hadn't been a rebel. Just lazy. He had demonstrated a congenital failure to expend any effort at anything that required work, including his music. And as Sarah quickly found out, "bursting the bonds" for Earl corresponded to an inability to maintain anything close to a monogamous relationship.

Zach, on the other hand, represented everything that was good and decent in Sarah's opinion. He was a yoga instructor, a terrific one given his ardent following. Not content to improve his employer's business, he had bravely struck out on his own six months ago, forming Grantham Yoga and Wellness Center. He knew the uncertainties, especially in the weak economy, but he had a solid business plan and was determined to reach for his dream. As part of his holistic approach, he had also brought in a nutritionist as a partner, and working as a team they had seen their clientele steadily increase.

Then, once his finances had started to stabilize, Zach had proposed.

And Sarah had accepted, not because she had felt over the moon—she had given up the whole over-the-moon stuff two months after moving in with Earl. No, she'd accepted because she had found contentment. Contentment was good.

Anyway, besides being financially stable, Zach was a good citizen—he coached in the local youth soccer league. *And* he was faithful. Zach never showed any inclination to wander despite all those women in sports bras and various forms of body-hugging knitwear.

So, in Sarah's view, he was free to lecture her for fifteen minutes on whatever he fancied. He could even take twenty.

Speaking of twenty minutes, Sarah glanced at her wrist. She knew it was neurotic to wear a watch on her wedding day—all right, not vaguely—but she couldn't help it. That was the type of person she had become. Besides, it *was* her grandmother's old Longines dress watch, so it was fulfilling the "something old" and "something borrowed" elements of the wedding ritual.

She finished fussing with her dress and turned to her mother. "Mom, I know you mean well, but why don't we just agree that you're happy to be able to share this day with me?" Sarah patted her mother sweetly on the upper arm of her jacket dress. Penny was wearing a beige mother-of-the-bride ensemble that she'd made from a Butterick pattern.

"All right, dear." Penny dabbed her eyes once more. "I'm just so happy, but I think I'd better warn you."

Sarah inhaled sharply.

"Your father did mention that he was planning on

bringing up something along the lines of you finally turning your life around—as part of his toast, that is."

Sarah groaned silently and placed her hand on her diaphragm. She pressed against the knot of indigestion that had taken up residence for the past few weeks. "I don't suppose there's any point in trying to talk to Dad ahead of time?" She looked at her mother's dubious expression. "No, I didn't think so. Well, I'm sure I have survived worse."

She glanced at her watch again. "You know, he won't get to say anything if I don't remind the groom that it's almost time. Zach is one of those people who never wears a watch, which is why he has me around, I guess." Sarah hoisted up the full skirt of her dress and headed for the door.

"Can't your father do that?" Penny said. "He's just outside trying to pick up the baseball game on that little transistor radio I bought him for our tenth wedding anniversary. It's practically a relic, but he insists it's still perfectly good, even if it did confuse the security man at the airport."

Sarah brushed past her mother. "Far be it from me to bother Dad before the seventh inning stretch." She strode down the narrow hallway. Her satin ballet slippers moved soundlessly along the stone floor. In deference to Zach's self-conscious concerns about being shorter, she had given up wearing anything remotely resembling heels. Even barefoot, the top of his head came just to her nose, and Sarah, all five-ten of her, had found herself compensating with a noticeable slump. As a physiotherapist, the poor posture irritated her no end. As a woman prepared to join her hand in holy matrimony, she had decided to compromise. She'd stand up straight at work and slump at home.

She reached the heavy wooden door to the chaplain's office and knocked. Zach had a habit of meditating in anticipation of stressful events, and she didn't want to interrupt any Zen-like trance too abruptly.

She didn't hear anything, so she knocked again.

Penny tiptoed next to her daughter. "Sarah, isn't it bad luck for the groom to see the bride before the wedding?"

"Don't be ridiculous." Sarah put her ear to the polished wood. "There's no such thing as bad luck." She called through the door, "Zach?"

She heard a muffled noise that sounded as if Zach had a cough drop lodged in his throat.

The strange muffled noise grew louder. She frowned. That didn't sound like a cough drop crisis. She placed her hand on the doorknob, pushed the door ajar and looked in.

She froze.

"Sarah, Sarah, is something wrong with Zach?" her mother asked.

Sarah turned to shield her mother. She drew the door shut. "Mom." She wet her lips, and then wet her lips again. "I think it might be better if I spoke to Zach alone." There was a quaver in her voice.

From the other side of the door, there was the sound of furniture creaking and rocking.

"Nonsense. I'm the mother of the bride. If anyone should talk to the groom, it should be me, by tradition. I know, you don't believe in these things, but I do. So, young lady, I don't know what's gotten into you, but I can see it's time I asserted a mother's prerogative."

Penny led with her shoulder past her trembling daughter. She might be all of five foot three and out of her element in an Ivy League setting, but nobody should underestimate Penny Halverson, she of sturdy Norwegian immigrant stock. She not only made lutefisk, she enjoyed it.

"Zach," her mother called, barging in. "It's Penny, and it's time you got…" Her voice trailed off. The creaking and rocking stopped.

Penny turned back to Sarah, her mouth ajar, pointing vaguely behind her.

Sarah nodded. The next thing she knew, her mother had crumpled to the floor.

"Oh, no." Sarah crouched next to her. "Mom?" She reached for her hand.

From down the hall, she could hear a tapping of heels. "Hey, Sarah, this is your matron of honor doing her sacred duty. The natives are starting to get restless out there, you know. I think it's time to get this show on the road." It was Katarina.

Sarah glanced up before quickly going back to holding her mother's limp hand. "There's been a slight delay in the action. My mother just fainted. Could you go get Julie?" She bent down. "Mom? Mom? Can you hear me?"

Muffled voices arose from the other side of the door. Then the sound of footsteps followed by a tentative knock. "Sarah," came a timid voice.

Sarah got up, turned the heavy iron key in the lock and pocketed it. She came back and squatted by her mother.

"What the…?" Katarina shifted her worried gaze from Penny to the sounds.

"Don't bother with that," Sarah said. "Just go get Julie. Mom may have hurt herself when she hit the deck."

Less than a minute later, an Amazon-like woman came running down the hallway, the straight skirt of her teal bridesmaid dress hiked up around her thighs, her dress sandals dangling from her fingertips. As soon as she saw Sarah and her mother on the floor, she skittered to a stop and dropped to her knees. Her bridesmaid's bouquet landed nearby.

Katarina followed closely behind. "How's your mom?"

"She's just starting to come to." She looked over at Julie. "Your stockings are mincemeat, you know."

"There're worse things in life, believe me," Julie said. She immediately redirected her focus to Penny. "Mrs. Halverson, can you hear me?"

Penny blinked her eyes slowly open and attempted to get up. "What…what happened?"

"Stay there, Mrs. Halverson. You fainted. I'm Sarah's friend Julie. You remember me?"

Penny nodded.

"I'm a doctor," Julie went on, her voice calm but authoritative. "I just want to check you out before you try to get up."

Penny swallowed. "I'm…I'm so embarrassed. I've never done anything like this before."

Julie peered into Penny's eyes and felt around her head and neck for bumps. "Do you remember what triggered the fainting?"

Sarah's head shot up. "Ah-h, I wouldn't go there if I were you."

Just then an argument seemed to erupt from the

other side of the door. Julie frowned. "What's going on in—"

Heavy footsteps coming down the hallway interrupted her words. "Is everyone all right?" It was Ben, Katarina's husband. Despite his oversize physique, he looked very smart in a custom-made tuxedo. Katarina must have put the screws to him because he'd even gone and gotten a haircut for the occasion.

Katarina put her hand up. "It's okay, sweetie. I think we've got it under control."

He looked at Penny lying slack in her daughter's arms. "Well, it doesn't look that way to me." His baritone was full-bodied.

Immediately, there was a large thump from the other side of the door, followed by more scurrying noises.

All heads turned, even Penny's.

Ben pushed his way toward the door.

Sarah stood. "No, let me." She brandished the key. "Julie, could you hold my mom?"

"Okay. But you're sure you don't want to let Ben check it out?"

Sarah sniffed, slipped her grandmother's watch up her wrist, and stepped around her mother. "No, I think it's more like cue the bride." She set her jaw, unlocked the wooden door and pushed it open.

Katarina and Julie craned their necks.

"Oh, my God! I don't believe it!" Katarina exclaimed loudly.

"What a total and utter schmuck!" Julie shouted.

A startled voice escaped from the other side of the door. "Sarah, I can explain."

"No, let me," came a second voice.

Ben took a step forward, but Sarah held out an arm.

"Oh-h-h…" Penny swooned for a second time. Luckily, Julie was still holding her.

Sarah closed the door, relocked it and faced her friends, leaning against the wall. "You saw what I saw, right?" Sarah looked from one face to another.

Katarina nodded. "If you mean that they were untangling their naked selves from a Revolving Half Moon Pose, I would have to agree."

Sarah bit her lip. "Actually, I think it was the Downward Facing Pigeon."

Ben coughed. "Where I come from, we don't need that many words to describe what they were doing. What I want to know is who's in there with Zach?"

Julie patted Sarah's mother on both cheeks to revive her.

"It's Ken, his partner in his yoga practice," Sarah said.

"Sarah?" the male voice on the other side of the door sounded plaintively.

Penny moaned.

Sarah looked down. "Mo-om…oh…Mo-om, I'm so sorry."

"Was, Zach with—with…another man?" Her mother was almost too frightened to ask. "Here? In Grantham?"

Julie blew air between her pursed lips. "And they would have still been going at it, totally oblivious to the outside world, if we hadn't made so much noise."

"Thank you for pointing that out," Sarah said. Silently, she rehashed her own lovemaking with Zach and came to the stark realization that they had never achieved such a passionate detachment from reality. Should that have been a clue? Who knew at this point? The only thing that was clear in her mind, *and* in her heart, was that she was broken. Utterly and absolutely broken. Crushed.

She placed her hand on her stomach to control yet another surge of indigestion. She tried to gather her thoughts, but the image of Zach and Ken kept interfering.

Still, she refused to come apart. She'd save that for later. "Well, let's see…we need a plan," she stated in a deliberate tone. "First…ah…the guests. They'll need to be told that the wedding is off—I should probably do that."

"I'm happy to do it." Katarina stepped forward.

Sarah bit down on her lower lip and nodded. "Thanks, but I think it's only proper that I should. In the meantime, could you let everyone know I plan to address them in a minute?" She looked over to Ben. "And could you do me a big favor? Could you go and tell my father the news? He's outside. I know I'm being a coward, but I don't think I could face him, not yet, anyway. And I certainly don't want him back here. Who knows what he'd do?"

Ben straightened his shoulders. "I'll be happy to. But first, with your permission, I'd like to deck Zach. I feel the need to inflict pain. You have to understand—it's a guy thing."

"It's not just a guy thing."

Her own gas pain reared up more violently. She breathed in deeply, if not a little noisily. It was New Jersey, after all, the pollen capital of America. "Thanks, Ben, you don't need to punch out Zach. Just dealing with my father will be more than enough," she said. She slanted her head toward the closed door. "First, I'll take care of business here, then I'll go tell the guests."

She studied her mother. Penny had started to sob quietly.

Sarah reached in the hidden pocket of her wedding dress and pulled out a hand-embroidered handkerchief. It had been Grammy's, as well. She handed it to Julie. "Here, you can pass this to my mom. I know she has one of her own, but this might be a source of added comfort." Grammy had been a sensible woman. She would have understood.

Next, without missing a beat, Sarah clasped her left hand and began working off the engagement ring that Zach had picked out and she had always found too showy. She passed it to Julie while Katarina busily positioned the bouquet of ferns and lilies of the valley under Penny's head to act as a cushion.

"Could you take this, too?" Sarah asked. "I don't want it to get in the way."

"The way?" Julie looked confused.

"I intend to slap a certain someone silly, but I have no desire to break any skin."

"Sarah. Let me explain. *Ple-ease.*" Zach's wailing voice penetrated through the door.

Sarah shook her head. "When I come back out, and after my mother has recovered—poor Mom—I'm not sure she'll ever recover. Earl was one thing, but this.... Anyhow, when all the drama's died down, do you think someone could scrounge me up some Tums?"

"Tums? I was thinking more along the lines of vodka," Katarina said.

Sarah laughed a sad laugh. "Actually, vodka sounds like a great idea, but under the circumstances, I'm afraid it's not such a good idea," she said in a low voice, not wanting to further upset her mother. Penny's eyelashes fluttered closed.

Katarina raised her eyebrows. "And that's because…"

"You remember when I told you how my father blew a gasket when he found out I was living with Earl in New York City?"

Katarina and Julie nodded.

"Well, he's going to have an apoplectic fit when he learns that this time I'm pregnant."

CHAPTER TWO

September, four months later

"RUN, FRED, RUN!" Huntington Phox called to the black-and-white dog that was dashing from one side of the backyard to the other. A mixture of Australian cattle dog and an undisclosed number of hounds, Fred was low to the ground and moved like a bullet train.

"Uh…Hunt, I think he's mastered running. It's 'stop' that might need a little more work." Ben Brown turned from watching the hyperactive animal to his longtime friend and partner.

He and Hunt went back more than a few years, first working at the same investment firm on Wall Street before Ben unnecessarily took the fall for an insider trading scandal and left the company. The two had gone on to found a successful venture capital firm in Grantham. Hunt knew that Ben was grateful. For his sticking by Ben no matter what, Hunt also knew his friend was more than grateful.

He also knew he was cagey. Ben might gladly walk through fire, walk on water, or put out the fire *with* the water for Hunt. But that didn't mean he didn't have his own agenda.

So Hunt waited, knowing that Ben was mindful of the tactical nuances necessary when it came to persuading

Hunt about something. Because, even though Hunt may have been born with a silver spoon in his mouth, he haggled with all the skill of a Bedouin horse trader.

"So when did you acquire this…this…beast?" Ben asked, opening with what Hunt surmised was a sideways gambit.

Hunt glanced at Ben before returning his attention to Fred. The "beast" raced along the winding paths fronting the flowerbeds, scattering pine-bark chips and beheading several black-eyed Susans.

"For your information, Fred happens to be a dog, a one-year-old dog, and I picked him up today when I was driving by the animal shelter."

"Well, if you say he's a dog, I guess I'll have to believe you. But he looks more like a big tail attached to an unidentified flying object."

Fred chose that moment to leap a hydrangea bush with a single bound. He made it about halfway before losing air and crashing into the branches. Ben winced. Fred bounced out and looked around. His tongue hung out, practically reaching his knuckles. His eyes were bright and eager.

Ben shook his head. "All I can say, you're a braver man than I to risk bringing a new puppy to your mother's garden."

Hunt turned. His hands were thrust into the pockets of the khaki pants that hung from his slim hips. He had finished his rounds of chemotherapy three months ago, but his weight loss was still apparent. Not that he had ever been heavy. But the lanky physique that had proved ideal for skiing and tennis and wearing a custom-made tuxedo with debonair flair, now resembled an undernourished teenager's. The bulky fisherman's knit sweater only accentuated his sunken chest. And the baseball cap he wore barely concealed his stubby hair, thinner and curlier than the thick blond waves he once had.

"It's not a question of bravery," Hunt said in response to Ben's remark. "I brought Fred here because my house doesn't have a fenced-in yard." That was true. His ultra-modern in-town dwelling might have a rooftop pool, a state-of-the-art sound system, and a well-stocked wine cellar, but it lacked even a single blade of grass.

He went back to admiring the dog's antics. "Besides, Mother won't know. She's in Manhattan, attending the opening of a new exhibit at the Met." Those of Hunt's social ilk only ever used the shortened form of the Metropolitan Museum of Art.

"And you think she won't notice when she gets back?" Ben watched as Fred finally gave up the chase and plopped down in a sunken reflecting pool. The mutt lapped the water, then raised his head and panted. Water dribbled from his corrugated black lips. He looked very wet, very tired and very proud.

Ben laughed.

Hunt shrugged. "I'll figure out something. In the meantime, I keep reminding myself that I am her only son and heir."

Ben walked over to the pond and looked more closely. "At the same time you might try reminding yourself that your mother's prized water garden used to be in that pond."

Fred burped. He waggled his narrow bottom on what was once a rare species of water lily.

Hunt winced.

Ben straightened up. "Although I don't have the name

of an exotic-plant specialist on speed dial, I'm not without some equally powerful resources. Lucky for you, I think I know how to smooth this over."

Hunt raised his eyebrows doubtfully. He had an inkling his friend was about to show his hand.

"Oh, ye of little faith." Ben pulled out a pamphlet from the back pocket of his jeans.

Hunt looked at it. "Don't tell me. Some little idea of my mother's?"

"What did you expect? She drove out to my place a few days ago and showed me the course listing for the new session of the Adult Education School. She thought you might be interested, and I agreed it was a good idea."

"She scared you witless, didn't she?"

Ben held up his hands. "Completely. Still, in my defense, after she left I stuffed the pamphlet in a pile of junk mail, never intending to talk to you about it. But now, given the circumstances…." He nodded toward Fred. A water lily pad adorned his forehead.

Hunt flipped open the front cover and read the introductory remarks in mocking tones,

"Dear Grantham Community Members,
Welcome to the twenty-sixth year of the Grantham Adult School! As in years past, we are delighted to offer a wide range of classes to meet the needs and interests of the community. Our instructors include noted scholars from Grantham University, as well as artists, artisans and business experts residing in the area. Above all, we at the Adult School believe that education does not

end with a diploma. Hence, our motto, Education: the Wellspring of Life.

Iris Phox, President
Grantham Adult School"

Hunt snapped the booklet shut. "As I recall, those very words practically made you gag not all that long ago."

"Yeah, I admit that's true. But think what it did for me. When I finally went—okay, not entirely on purpose—to Katarina's class, I found the woman I love, got my relationship with my son back in order, and acquired a whole new set of friends and family. That's what I call adult education!"

Hunt slipped his hand in his pants pocket and pulled out his BlackBerry.

"Who are you calling?" Ben asked.

"Oprah. Your story needs to be told to a larger audience."

Ben rolled his eyes. "Okay, okay. I know it sounds hokey. But that doesn't mean it's not a smart thing to do. I mean, look at you. You just hang around doing nothing. You're not interacting with anyone except... except some mutt whose social skills leave more than a little to be desired."

"I presume you are referring to my friendship with you?" Hunt joked.

"All right, I asked for that. Not all of us were born on the right side of the tracks."

Hunt knew that Ben's declaration grossly understated the harshness of his childhood years.

"But say what you will, at least I'm working my butt off to earn an honest living," Ben continued.

Hunt rubbed his cheek. "I thought you were okay with me taking a leave from work. If you've changed your mind, then you're free to get a new partner."

"Jeez, Hunt, I don't *want* a new partner. And I'm perfectly okay with you taking time off. What I'm not okay with is you taking a leave of absence from life. I mean, to tell you the truth, I just don't get it. When you were first diagnosed with lymphoma and had to go through all that wretched treatment, you were amazing, more than amazing. I still can't believe how you insisted on coming in practically every day while you were undergoing chemo, let alone dealing with the stress and worry. But now that it's behind you, you're a wreck. Logic tells me it should be the other way around."

Hunt frowned. "There're those people who can't cope with the prospect of death. For me, it's the prospect of living that's got me stymied."

"Well, just get out there and join the human race. If I can do it, you can! I mean, we all know how hopeless I am when it comes to remembering names and making polite small talk."

"Let alone impolite small talk."

Ben pointed at his friend. "See! You're witty even when you're not trying! My God, you could practically charm a doorknob!"

"And don't think I haven't."

"So think how many *more* doorknobs are out there awaiting your unique talents." Ben noticed the dog in his peripheral vision. "Besides, if what I'm saying doesn't convince you, I'm pretty sure Fred here will." He nodded in Fred's direction. "Don't look now, but I think you'll find there's something shiny hanging out the side of his mouth, something finlike."

Hunt rushed over to the reflecting pool. "Holy crap, Fred!" He slapped the pamphlet he was still holding against his pants to get the dog's attention. "That's one of Mother's prized koi. She's going to kill you." Fred bit down proudly. There was a noticeable crunch.

"Your mother would never kill an animal. She's on the board of the Grantham animal shelter. I know because she hit me up for a large donation," Ben said.

Hunt rubbed his mouth. "You're right. Fred, I think you're going to live." He turned slowly back to Ben. "Do you think Mother would hit a recent cancer victim?"

Ben crossed his arms, looking very pleased, indeed. "With gusto. During her visit she was telling me how much she enjoyed the class on weight lifting to prevent osteoporosis."

Hunt took off his baseball cap, and ran his hand through the thin strands. "Then the only way to get out of this…" He reluctantly looked down at the Adult School listing.

"Exactly."

Hunt raised his eyes. "And I suppose she already has a course in mind?"

Ben scoffed. "You doubted that for a second?"

"Tell me it's a large lecture where I can hide in the back of the room," Hunt implored.

"I could tell you that, but…"

Hunt closed his eyes. "Okay, tell me the truth. I'm man enough to take it."

"It's a water aerobics class. Here, give me back the course listing, and I'll read you the details."

"Water aerobics?" Hunt grimaced and held out the pamphlet.

Ben flipped the pages. "Here it is. 'Light Water Aerobics. This six-week class is designed for pregnant women, older citizens and those recovering from injuries, or those wanting a lighter, low-impact workout. Meets Wednesdays, 7:30 p.m., Grantham Middle School Swimming Pool.'" Ben closed the booklet. "See, it sounds perfect."

Hunt frowned. "If it's so perfect, why don't you sign up for it?"

"Because I'm not pregnant, old—"

Hunt snorted.

"Excuse me, thirty-eight is not old. Nor am I recovering from an injury. Besides, I know from Katarina's experience that her knee rehabbed really well in the water. I mean, what have you got to lose?"

Hunt rubbed his lips again. They were perennially chapped despite a constant application of lip balm. "I don't know. My dignity? Besides, six weeks? That's kind of a long commitment."

"I've got news for you. Getting a dog isn't exactly a short-term affair either—right, Fred?"

Hearing his name, the dog sat up in a way that for any other dog might be considered majestic. On Fred, it emphasized the fact that his head seemed to belong to a breed completely unrelated to the rest of his body.

Suddenly inspired, Fred jumped out of the pool and shook himself all over Hunt.

Hunt brushed the water off his pants. "This affair could be shorter than you think. I wouldn't say he's exactly ingratiating himself." He bent down to grab the leash lying on the flagstones and reached for the dog's webbed canvas collar. Not quickly enough, though.

Fred was off and running again, this time through a stand of hibiscus.

Hunt stared gloomily at the leash hanging limply in his hand. "So what do I have to do to join this class?"

"Nothing…well…practically nothing. Your mother has already enrolled you. All you need to do is show up tomorrow night, with a bathing suit and towel. How hard can that be?"

Hunt sighed as Fred moved on from rummaging through the hibiscus to trampling the fragile pale pink flowers of fall-blooming cyclamen. "Tell me, do you think Mother has any pâté in the house?"

"Why? Are you feeling peckish?" Ben asked.

"No, I'm looking for something to bribe the dog with to get him to come. And knowing Mother, she won't have anything as mundane as liverwurst."

Ben laughed. "I'm sure there must be some imported Brie." Then he glanced down at his watch. "I'd stay and help, but I'm already late for picking up Matt from school. The only thing worse than seeing *your* mother angry is seeing *my* teenage son pissed off."

"And you call yourself a friend?" Hunt teased. "Oh, all right, far be it from me to cause any family dis-harmony. And just to show you how cooperative I can be, I'll make nice with Mother and attend this water-whatever class."

"Light Water Aerobics." Ben sidestepped to the gate. He rested his hand on the latch. "Hunt, one more thing…"

Hunt was busy weaving and bobbing, trying to out-maneuver the dog. Fred let him come to just beyond arm's length. Hunt lunged. Fred scampered away. Hunt swore.

"Hunt?" Ben said again.

"I know, I know, tomorrow night. Seven-thirty. I'll be there."

Ben paused. "Do you want me to leave the course listing?"

Hunt waved him off. "Don't bother. I think you pretty much hit the highlights."

"If you say so," Ben agreed. He left quickly—Hunt couldn't help thinking—curiously relieved.

CHAPTER THREE

WEDNESDAYS WERE ALWAYS a bitch as far as Sarah was concerned. She closed her eyes and rubbed her lower back. This particular Wednesday was proving to be beyond bitchy.

She turned her head and eyed the seventy-year-old woman next to her who was adjusting the plunging neckline of her bathing suit. For someone her age, she looked fantastic. Okay, she had the usual upper arm waddle and her thighs, while toned, showed signs of cellulite. But, hey, Sarah wouldn't mind having that body at that age. Even half her age for that matter.

Sarah looked down at her swollen belly with its spidery stretch marks. "Wanda, do you really think a bikini is the way to go?" Thirty weeks along in her pregnancy, she was exhibiting all the expected signs, like clockwork.

Talk about stretch marks. Besides her belly, pink and purple lines now etched her breasts and inner thighs. Lovely. Then there was her belly button, which had gone from being an innie to a full-blown outie.

All those women who positively glowed in pregnancy? Not Sarah. Her cheeks might be flushed, but pimples had a way of erupting daily on her chin and the tip of her nose. She had found this incredibly expensive "nighttime eruption solution" that seemed to help. A little.

Sarah rubbed her swollen belly and told herself to quit being cranky. After all, it was all worth it, right? Still, just because she could accept the changes in her body didn't mean she felt obliged to flaunt them. "Maybe I could wear a T-shirt over the bikini top?" she said.

Wanda grabbed the combination lock from her tote bag and slammed the metal locker shut. "Nonsense, baby bumps are all the rage now, isn't that right, Lena?" Wanda turned to her good friend. Lena was Wanda's tennis partner as well as Katarina's grandmother.

Lena adjusted the strap of her bathing cap under her chin. "What's that? Who's right?" Lena patted Sarah protectively on her arm. "Never mind. You would look wonderful wearing a burlap bag. And in that suit—" she raised her arms, hands open "—you are the image of a Rubens beauty in all your womanly glory."

Sarah twisted her neck around. "Are you trying to tell me that my butt looks fat?" She gripped one cheek in an assessment.

"Nonsense, dear," Wanda said. "You're every woman's dream—a long-stemmed American beauty, curvy like the legs of a Chippendale table, and with breasts the size of cantaloupes. That's why we all agreed that the bikini was absolutely, positively the right choice."

Sarah shook her head. "Thanks, I think." She was still trying to wrap her head around the image of Chippendale furniture and cantaloupes until she decided it was just another strange moment in an already eventful day.

Because at the end of a full schedule of running multiple physical therapy sessions, three of Sarah's late Wednesday afternoon clients had thrown her a surprise baby shower. They included Wanda, a retired high school math teacher, who was having treatments for the tendonitis in her tennis arm. "I know it would probably get better if I developed a two-handed backhand, but at my age…"

Lena was there, too, a sturdy fireplug of a woman who when she spoke still had a hint of her native Czechoslovakia in her accent. Her arthritic knees had started to act up on her. Too many years of standing up at her hardware store and playing tennis. She'd had some arthroscopic surgery over the summer to clean up one knee, and was now diligently doing her rehab.

Rounding out the group was Rufus Treadway. A mainstay of the local African-American community, Rufus had had a hip replacement about a year ago. Unfortunately, he was not yet tripping the light fantastic, which was a real shame, as far as Sarah was concerned. So she'd pulled some strings and got him an appointment with the hip specialist at the University of Pennsylvania Hospital.

Anyhow, when the three of them had pulled out the streamers and party blowers, Sarah had been truly taken aback. Lena had made a plum tart. "Not to worry. It's mostly fruit," she had said.

And butter and eggs, Sarah had thought.

When they next produced several wrapped boxes, she was overwhelmed. "You shouldn't have," Sarah protested, expecting to get several hand-knitted baby sweaters and maybe a baby-size Grantham University baseball cap.

"Start with the squishy one," Wanda insisted.

Sarah carefully removed the wrapping paper—no

sense in wasting perfectly good paper when it could be reused—and found a Speedo bathing cap.

"How lovely. I don't have one," Sarah said, confused but careful to affix a smile.

"Now the flat one." Rufus pointed to an oblong wrapped box.

That one yielded flip-flops. Another had a rolled up beach towel.

Sarah laughed. "I think I see a theme here. I know I always tout the virtues of swimming as a low-impact exercise for you all, so I'm glad to see the message is getting across."

Then came the biggest box. It seemed to contain mostly tissue paper, but buried deep inside Sarah found a maternity bathing suit in electric orange. A teeny-tiny, two-piece maternity suit. "I didn't know they made bikinis for pregnant women." She held up the top and bottom to universal clapping.

And last but not least, Rufus pulled out a slim envelope.

"A ticket to the Bahamas?" Sarah joked. She slit the envelope open and read the contents, "This confirms your registration in the Adult School 'Light Water Aerobics' class for pregnant woman and those rehabilitating from injuries.'"

"Isn't it great!" Wanda had exclaimed. "It's tonight, and Lena and I have signed up, too! It'll be like a continuation of our workouts here!" Then she squealed.

That should have been a tip-off, Sarah thought as she now stood in the women's locker room on the second floor of the Grantham Middle School. Goose bumps appeared on more exposed skin than she cared to think about. She picked up her towel from the bench and wrapped it around her waist. There might be less of her on display to the world, but she was afraid she now looked like a beached whale in terry cloth.

Indeed, the whole idea of lowering her inflated body into a chlorinated swimming pool was just not all that appealing to her at the moment. Any sane person in a similar circumstance would be home, curled up in a comfy chair, watching the rerun of Comedy Central's *Daily Show* and eating a grilled-cheese sandwich, better yet, mocha-chip ice cream straight out of the container.

"C'mon, dear, you don't want to be late. If you think I'm a stickler for punctuality, wait till you meet Doris," Wanda said.

Sarah scooped up her bathing cap and obeyed. So much for sanity. She followed Wanda and Lena down the stairs and, mindful of her manners, she held open the door to the pool area for the older women first. *Wham!* The heat and humidity assaulted her immediately. The smell of chlorine just about brought up the plum cake.

Sarah looked down and gulped. Finally, she risked lifting her head—and got her first look at the pool. "Wanda, I thought this class was for women only?"

"Whatever gave you that idea?" Wanda asked all innocent.

Sarah looked around again. Three other women in various stages of pregnancy were there, none of them wearing bikinis. *Great.* She also couldn't help noticing that they all had male partners in tow.

The couples clustered together in a circle, tight enough that a take-out *venti* couldn't fit in between. As Sarah walked by, she could hear them exchanging due dates and giggles. Men-and-women giggles.

Wanda and Lena moved to the side of the couples group, where they joined an older man with a vertical scar down his chest. Bypass surgery. Next to him was another man who looked to be in his fifties, almost a carbon copy of the older guy except with more hair, considerably less weight, and a hollow look in his eyes and cheeks. Father and son seemed to be old friends of Wanda and Lena, since the four of them…well…mostly the three of them, were chatting it up. The son appeared to hang at the fringes nodding at appropriate times, but adding little to the conversation.

She was about to join them and introduce herself when the buzzer sounded, signaling the start of class. The instructor, clipboard in hand, with a whistle hanging from a lanyard around her neck and reading glasses halfway down her nose, strode to the edge of the pool. She might be pushing sixty, but she looked like she could wrestle a grizzly bear with one hand tied behind her back while teaching the fundamentals of lifesaving with the other. She blew her whistle. The giggling and whispers halted.

"Good evening, everyone. I'm Doris Freund, your instructor for Light Water Aerobics," she announced. "Why don't I call the roll before we get down to business." She started rattling off names with marine sergeant precision, and when she was partway down the list she called out, "Halverson, Sarah." She peered over her reading glasses.

Sarah waved. "Pres—"

The door to the pool swung open. Doris looked up at the clock. Everyone else stared at the door.

Sarah immediately saw a man, and from his surfer's shorts, lanky walk and thin frame assumed he was of college age. But after a quick glance at his face, she realized he was older—mid-thirties. He had the kind of features—sharp, high cheek bones, deep-set ice-blue eyes with lines fanning out at the corners, and a wide mouth with thin lips—that hinted at intelligence, wit, and, okay, *might as well admit it,* Sarah said to herself, long-term sex appeal. But there was also an air of mystery, or maybe it was sadness. Which only made him more intriguing. But truth be told, the physical attribute that had caught her attention was that he was thin. Very thin, on a frame that could use an extra twenty pounds.

Cancer and the side effects of chemotherapy. Pretty rough. He was young and as an expectant father…

Sarah waited, watching the door, wondering what his wife would look like. Only nobody came. She raised an eyebrow. So if he wasn't an expectant father…

She saw him glance quickly around and stop. His mouth opened, but no words came forth. He surveyed the group slowly, then screwed up his mouth.

"I find as a rule that the class works better if we all arrive on time," Doris said sternly. "I've scheduled a number of activities, and to maximize the benefits and everyone's enjoyment I'd prefer not to have to rush any of them, if you catch my drift?" She waited for an acknowledgment.

The latecomer breathed in and lifted his head, elevating his proud chin. "Duly noted," he said. He blinked. "Mrs. Montgomery?"

"Huntington? Huntington Phox, is that really you? I haven't seen you since you were in fifth grade."

"Fourth," he said.

Doris arched one brow critically.

"Well, maybe you're right. Fifth." He didn't sound convinced but obviously was astute enough to know when to give in. "And most people call me Hunt now," he said.

"Yes, well, Huntington, it's good to see you after all this time. But it's not Mrs. Montgomery anymore. Mr. Montgomery passed away some twenty years ago."

"Sorry to hear that."

"And then there was Mr. Dunworth." Her voice took a reflective tone. "He was a merchant marine. But you know how they are. So now it's back to Ms. Freund, my maiden name. But everyone may of course call me Doris."

LIKE THAT WAS ABOUT TO HAPPEN, Hunt thought. He noticed that all the class members nodded nervously, all except this one tall woman with straight dark-blond hair that she was attempting to squeeze into a racing cap.

Under other circumstances he might have admired her fine features, but these were not exactly normal circumstances.

How normal could it be given the fact that he was forced to stand in front of a bunch of strangers, not to mention his former grammar school teacher, wearing the only pair of swim trunks he had managed to find in the bottom of his dresser drawer. Not just any trunks, either, but some faded board shorts, half-forgotten mementos from a surfing vacation during his junior year spring break.

But enough about his laughable figure—too bad he wasn't laughing—since his attention anyway was fixated on this real-life grown-up female. Wearing a bright orange bikini that barely held her bountiful curves.

Hunt blinked, amazed that here at the Grantham Middle School swimming pool of all places, the embers of sexual urges long dormant—one of the many side effects of chemo that didn't really compute until you experienced them—had suddenly started to smolder. Talk about less than normal circumstances.

And the smoldering was especially bizarre given that her little scraps of stretchy material did nothing to hide the fact that not only did she have the breasts of a pinup, she also was very pregnant—very, very pregnant.

Hunt cleared his throat and turned to address Ms. Freund, or rather, Doris. "Please do not take this personally if I slip up now and again. I seem to find it difficult to call my fourth, no, fifth grade teacher by her first name."

Doris clucked. "You're your mother's son, that's for sure."

There were some twitters, and Hunt searched out the source of the laughter. He recognized Lena Zemanova, the grandmother of Ben's wife. The sprightly seventy-something-year-old wore a no-nonsense racing suit, navy with white piping, and a red bathing cap. She looked ready to swim the English Channel. The woman next to her, with spiky black hair and a leathery tan that spoke of years of retirement and a complete disregard for sun block, also looked familiar. Though Hunt couldn't quite place her, unless…unless…. He raised his eyebrows.

"That's right, Huntington," she replied with a snap of her gum. "I'm your worst nightmare. Wanda Garrity, your high school math teacher from freshman year. And I'm still waiting for your problem set on quadratic equations."

Hunt caught sight of her pierced belly button, visible

through the large silver ring holding together her low-cut silver swimsuit. He closed his eyes. "I'll have it for you next week."

"Well, now that we're all here, why don't I explain how the course works," Doris went on in full lecture mode. "As you know from the course description, this class is designed to provide a low-impact aerobic workout. I promise to raise your heart rate in a way that will not tax your joints but instead strengthen your muscles. We're also going to work on flexibility and strength exercises that are appropriate to your conditions, whether recuperative or reproductive."

Doris waited. "Does everyone understand?"

A MIASMA OF CHLORINE-INFUSED air produced a rainbow glow around the wall lights. Moisture clung to the white tiles like a sheen of sweat. Sarah patted the back of her neck. Now that she was here, she was ready to get on with things.

Lena leaned across and nudged Sarah. "I'm excited but a little nervous. What about you?" She smiled.

Sarah smiled back at Lena's bright blue eyes, sparkling with encouragement. "I feel the same," she said.

"And you're sure you're not achy and tired after so long a day? I worry, you know," Lena said.

Sarah leaned down and whispered, "Not to worry. I'm glad I'm here."

"Good things will come of it, I promise," Lena told her.

"Excuse me." Doris gave them an evil look and went on with various bureaucratic details, like how to notify her if they had to miss a class and the policy on makeups, until finally she put her clipboard and reading glasses on a low bench by the wall. "So, if there are no questions or further interruptions—" she eyed Lena "—why don't we all get in the water? Congregate in the shallow end and find your partner." Doris brought her whistle to her mouth and gave an emphatic blow.

They shuffled to the end of the pool. Some of the couples jumped in. Spray splashed up. Giggles arose again, as the pregnant women floated, their bellies giving them terrific buoyancy. Carl, the older gentleman from earlier, used the ladder and steps on the side. Lena and Wanda squatted down and slipped in from the water's edge. Lena immediately got wet all over. Wanda was careful not to get her hair wet.

Finally, all twelve members of the class were in the water.

Except for two.

Sarah and Hunt stood by the water's edge, seemingly frozen to the tiled floor.

Doris sniffed. She was at the side of the pool ready to make a formal entry. "Is something wrong?" she asked.

"Partner? Did you say something about everyone having a partner?" Sarah said.

HUNT SHIFTED HIS EYES between the woman in the electric-orange bikini and Ms. Freund. "No one told me about a partner, either."

Doris *tsk-tsked* and slid into the water gracefully. "Didn't you read your course book?" She managed to look down her nose despite standing below them in the shallow end.

Sarah shook her head. "No, I...ah...friends enrolled me in the class without giving me all the details."

"I've got much the same story," Hunt added.

"Well, then you two will just have to pair up," Doris said. She turned to the rest of the class. "Let's do some gentle bobbing as a warm-up."

Hunt frowned. He looked at Sarah. "One of your friends wouldn't happen to be my mother, would it?"

"I don't know. Who's your mother?"

"Iris Phox."

"*The* Iris Phox?"

"So you know her?" he said.

"Well, *of* her. You can't live in Grantham without having heard of her." She sought out Lena in the pool. Her bathing cap bobbed up and down. "Lena, do you need a partner?"

Lena pointed to her right. "I'm with Wanda." Wanda was bobbing up and down. Whatever gel she had applied to her hair kept the spikes perfectly in place.

"I guess I don't measure up to your idea of a partner," Hunt said casually. Not that he was looking to be anybody's partner, but if there was going to be a rejection handed out, he found himself annoyed that he had been the one to be dumped.

Sarah turned to him. "Listen, it's nothing personal, but these days I don't do men partners."

"You have something against men?"

She shrugged. "Hypothetically, no. In practice, yes."

He made a gesture toward her protruding belly. "Does that mean you used in vitro?"

She protruded her lower lip and blew upward, sending her bangs flying. "I should have been so lucky."

"You two," Doris called out from the pool. "No dillydallying."

"We could both just leave," she said under her breath.

"And have my mother find out? I don't think so. On second thought, maybe *you* could explain it to my mother?"

"I don't think so. I'm not even sure I could explain it to *my* friends, especially when two of them are eyeing me from the water right now." She waved at Wanda and Lena. Then she turned back to Hunt. "I guess we have no choice."

Hunt sighed. "I suppose you're right. In which case, shall we?" He brought his hand forward in a gesture of invitation.

"I'm Sarah, by the way," she said.

"Hunt."

She dipped one toe in the water.

He noticed she used pearl-pink nail polish.

"I've got to warn you, though," she said.

"You don't swim?" he asked.

"No, I swim all right. But if you're looking for a partner to square things away with Wanda, I'm not much help. I don't remember a thing about quadratic equations." She jumped in the water and waded toward Wanda.

Hunt followed, sinking immediately. He bobbed up and wiped the water from his eyes. "And here I was counting on you to save my butt," he said, joining her.

Wanda cracked her gum. "If you only knew."

CHAPTER FOUR

"IT WAS HUMILIATING," Sarah blurted out. She wandered around the reception area of the salon in the nearby little town of Craggy Hill, looking at the wide array of OPI nail polishes on display. The salon was located on the first floor of an old frame house, with the cozy, cream-colored carpeted living room serving as the reception. Small back bedrooms worked perfectly as private spa facilities for pedicures, manicures, facials and massages.

Katarina and Julie were treating Sarah and themselves to pedicures as a prelude to the official baby shower that evening at Katarina and Ben's house.

"I'm sure you're exaggerating," Julie said. She was inspecting the line of France-themed colors, turning each bottle to read the label. "Ooh La La Lavender?" she asked to no one in particular. "A must for the fashion-conscious obstetrician on the go-go."

Katarina checked out the bottles lined up on the mantel. "I never knew there were so many types of clear polish. All right, I'll take the plunge and go for Shell Pink Shimmy." She clutched the bottle and turned to Sarah who was wriggling around in a club chair, trying to find a comfortable position. "And what about you, Woman of the Hour?" She leaned her head in the direction of Sarah. "What color will allow you to recover from the humiliation of water aerobics?"

"As if it matters? I'm so big I can barely see my feet." As if to prove her point, Sarah raised one leg just to get a good look at her sneaker. "So *that's* my right foot. Somehow I remember it being smaller."

"Well, what color is the bathing suit they got you for your class? You could go for that complete ensemble look," Katarina suggested with what seemed to be sincerity.

"Are you trying to be cruel? It was more like *in*complete ensemble. Do you know how little the top part of a bikini covers a pregnant woman's boobs?"

"I'd give anything to have boobs like yours. Why am I the only Italian-American woman I know who is flat as a pancake?" Julie asked.

"Please, let's not get into body issues. You, after all, have not entered the world of elastic-waist pants." Sarah glanced over at the selection of the new Spanish-themed nail polishes grouped atop a gateleg table. "What about that one?" She pointed to a deep pinkish-red one on the right.

"Wow!" Katarina walked over and picked up the bottle Sarah had indicated. "Conquistadorable. You have someone in mind to conquer?"

Sarah waved off the suggestion. "It's more like I think it matches the cherry pie I baked."

Julie shook her head. "That's our Sarah. Bakes a pie for her own baby shower."

"Well, I just wanted to help out. You guys have done so much on top of working and all. Besides, it's my way of relaxing," Sarah said.

And her way of connecting to her roots. Only she didn't say that.

Sarah might have run away from rural Minnesota as soon as she turned eighteen, but it didn't mean it was out of her system. True, when she'd followed Earl and become a rock band groupie, she'd gone completely "gonzo"—inky-black nails and purple-dyed hair, plus the requisite tongue piercing and studded neck collar. She'd lost her farm girl glow by staying up all night and bartending at clubs catering to local bands that sporadically favored Earl's erratic bass playing. But no amount of cheering improved Earl's musical ability, and it never kept him from straying.

Eager to redeem herself in her parents' eyes, she became a determined student/working girl. She'd enrolled at Hunter College's School of Health Professions, commuting to Manhattan from her dumpy apartment in Queens. This time she strove for upward mobility. She switched to bartending at Upper East Side haunts frequented by investment bankers and female interns at Sotheby's. Sarah had let her hair go back to her natural blond. She learned about button-down collars from the men and artists like Cy Twombly and Helen Frankenthaler from the women. At the same time she racked up a sizable debt for tuition bills, which dismayed her parents yet again when they realized the financial straits she had landed herself in.

So she tried again. Armed with a degree in physical therapy, she gravitated to Grantham for its college town atmosphere and close proximity to New York. And in an area populated by families with sports-happy kids, weekend warriors and aging retirees, the physical therapy business was booming. After first working at a large rehab facility, she landed her current job with a practice affiliated with the hospital. She liked the variety, and liked the feeling that she could follow the progress of a stroke victim from the hospital to at-home care through outpatient appointments at the office.

But still Penny regularly asked, "Is it true that most people in New Jersey are Italian? Not that I have anything against Italians. After all, your father and I enjoy eating pizza at the firehouse fundraisers."

Zach's most favorable qualities in her mother's eyes had been that he wasn't Earl, and that he'd proposed to their only daughter, just when they'd given up hope.

Now, though, Sarah knew she was truly disappointing them. It was one thing to be an unmarried mother-to-be, but it was another to have left your gay fiancé at the altar. She wondered how Penny explained that one at the firehouse fundraisers.

So here she was, soon to be a hardworking single mother. And while she told everybody that this is what she wanted to do with her life, there were many moments when she wondered, "Is this who I *really* want to be?"

At least she had baking to keep her company. Besides the cherry pies, there were the peach cobblers, the pineapple upside-down cakes and the snickerdoodles. The trick was to find other people to eat the baked goods so that her ever-expanding waistline was at least somewhat manageable.

Rather than rehash her inability to plot a straight and self-fulfilling course for her life, she decided to give herself a break. To enjoy the sensation of sitting down and knowing that nothing more strenuous awaited her than letting someone else pamper her for a while. Feeling a bit light-headed, she closed her eyes and rested her head on the back of the chair.

"You know, guys, this was a great idea to get pedicures. But I feel guilty."

Julie looked up from checking the messages on her iPhone. "When have we heard that before?"

Sarah opened her eyes. "Please tell me you'll let me help pay."

"Absolutely not!" Katarina protested.

"I know. You can bake the pedicurist some brownies," Julie said.

"What a good idea," agreed Sarah.

Julie dropped her head in her hand. "Tell me she's not serious."

"Sarah, don't even think of it. It's our treat. You see, I was reading online that the third trimester is the time to indulge in girly things," Katarina said, and grabbed a chair next to Sarah. "Besides, this gives Ben a chance to clean up the empty Cheetos bags and dirty socks and running shoes before the 'Big Event.'" She made little quotation marks with her fingers.

Sarah swallowed. Just the thought of Cheetos and smelly socks was enough to make her nauseated.

"What I wouldn't give for a bag of Cheetos now," Julie said. She scrounged around in her hobo purse on the floor and came up with a packet of Reese's Peanut Butter Cups.

"Can I tempt anyone?" she offered. Katarina and Sarah shook their heads, and Julie wasted no time consuming the candy. How the woman managed to live off junk food and still remain rail-thin was a mystery to Sarah.

The owner, Erika, approached them. "Well, ladies,

we have one room ready now, and the next two will be free in a few minutes. Who wants to go first?" Her voice had that melodious lilt of some unidentifiable Eastern European language. Her skin was flawless, as well. Clearly, there was something about sour cream, cabbage and potatoes.

Katarina held out a hand toward her friend. "Sarah, I don't want to hear any objections. This is your evening after all."

"It may be her evening, but she still hasn't given us the gory details about *yesterday's* water aerobics partner." Julie stopped munching and texting long enough to speak. "Though considering the pool of candidates who would have signed up—yes, I meant that terrible pun—it can't have been anyone all that interesting."

"Oh, he was all right," she said with a shrug.

All right?! her inner voice objected. *Tell them about Hunt Phox's steady stream of irreverent banter, how it had helped to pass the ninety minutes of class with surprising ease,* it demanded impatiently.

Because then I'd have to tell them that not only was he trying to allay our mutual awkwardness, but that fifteen minutes into the workout of stretching and bouncing with Styrofoam noodles and floats, the guy was exhausted.

So what?

Because it was clear from his determined look that he didn't want to be babied, didn't want to admit his limitations.

So?

So I respect his pride and his privacy.

Respect nothing. You call the tingling sensation you

felt when he gripped your forearms during isometric exercises "respect"?

"Earth to Sarah," Julie called, interrupting her internal debate. "Are you still with us?"

Sarah shook her head. "I'm so sorry. I didn't mean to flake out there. My thoughts just kind of got away from me. Chalk it up to general tiredness and pregnancy muddleheadedness, I guess." She blinked a few times, warding off the light-headedness she was feeling. It was a little hot in the shop.

Then she gripped the arms of the chair. "I really have been looking forward to this all day. It's just the logistics of getting up that seem a bit daunting." She pressed down to hoist herself up.

Which is when a weird thing happened.

Because instead of heaving herself into an upright position, Sarah became strangely conscious, almost out-of-body conscious, of pitching forward. And her nose—it really was her nose and not someone else's she kept thinking—seemed to be getting closer and closer to the rug. *This isn't part of the playbook,* she told herself.

And that thought came right before her left temple made contact with the cream-colored rug.

CHAPTER FIVE

HUNT FILLED THE VASE with water from the sink in Ben's kitchen, turned off the tap, and ambled over to the table, careful not to lose any of the hydrangea branches that jostled against each other. He placed the vase in the center of the wooden farm table and fussed inexpertly at the heavy blooms, the globes of dusty-blue flowers drooping toward the table.

"There, that should do it," he said, and backed away. "I thought I should bring something to Katarina if I was going to drop in."

"She's not here right now to thank you." Ben leaned against the kitchen counter, his arms crossed, and watched Hunt's efforts with a skeptically raised brow. "The dog trashed another bush in your mother's yard, didn't he? And you're just trying to hide the evidence, right?"

Hunt shrugged. "Well, something good might as well come from Fred's enthusiastic communing with nature. Besides, I think she was returning from her book group by six, and I didn't want her to look out the window and notice the damage. I made it with plenty of time to spare, I think." He instinctively glanced at his wrist before he remembered that he had stopped wearing one right after he'd finished chemo and no longer had to get to appointments on time.

No matter, he slipped his hand in the side pocket of his chinos for his BlackBerry. Nothing. Well, that suited him just fine. This was the New Hunt, the Stress-Free Hunt. He started to whistle off-key. The noise caused Fred to lift his head from licking the tile floor around the rubbish bin. He stared at his master with a wrinkled brow that might mistakenly be interpreted as intelligence. Then he scampered out of the kitchen with an unfocused sense of purpose.

"He's not going to do anything destructive, is he?" Ben asked. He watched Fred bolt down the hallway, his four paws barely touching the hardwood planks.

"He's fine. As long as you don't have any exotic fish in the house, I wouldn't worry."

"I'll be sure to keep the cans of tuna fish under wraps." Ben kept his arms crossed and waited.

"Listen, I've been doing a lot of thinking."

"Sometimes a wise move," Ben said sardonically.

Hunt continued undeterred. "I've come to the realization that I want to do something to help mankind. Make a difference for humanity."

"That's great." Ben uncrossed his arms. "Let me ask you, though. In the process of all your thinking, have you narrowed it down a little? Thought of anything in particular?"

Hunt wagged one finger in the air. "Not yet, but that will come. The crucial thing for now is that I am thinking about what I want to do."

Fred chose that moment to rush back into the kitchen. A white athletic sock hung from the corner of his mouth. He checked that Hunt was still there before twirling around and racing out again, the sock streaming behind his flopping ear.

Ben headed after the mutt. "You're lucky that I'm pretty sure that sock was Matt's." He walked to the bottom of the steep stairs leading to the second-floor bedrooms.

The eighteenth-century cottage had originally consisted of little more than the kitchen, but it had been expanded in the late nineteenth century to include a living room, dining room and a study on the ground floor. The attic had been refitted into two bedrooms at roughly the same time. The upstairs and downstairs bathrooms didn't come until the twentieth century, and Ben had recently updated them again.

"You know, Hunt, I was more than happy to renovate the bathrooms as a measure of my love and devotion to my lovely wife, but I hadn't counted on refinishing the stairs." He winced as the dog's nails scurried frantically on the wood as he bounded up the stairs, made a tight circle around the landing, and threw himself headfirst down once more. He stopped only to deposit the sock at Ben's feet before charging up yet again.

Ben turned to Hunt who had followed him, still muttering something about humanity. "You know, I'm going to bill you for the damage, and no amount of Adult School attendance is going to get you out of it." Ben shook his head in disgust.

Hunt smiled as he watched Fred repeat his frantic maneuvers. "Give him a break. He's never used stairs before."

"Poor baby. To have to live in a house with an elevator must be such a deprivation."

"That was the architect's idea, not mine. He called it 'an elegant solution to a challenging space.' His way of saying my downtown Grantham lot was way narrower than he originally realized, and why not spend another twenty grand or so on my modern folly." Hunt marveled at the dog's fierce glee. "Can you imagine the utter joy he must be feeling at experiencing something for the first time? To be that exhilarated, that overcome with emotion." He turned to Ben. "Can you remember a similar feeling? I know I can't. It must be like an awakening…like experiencing birth all over again."

"Listen, I can appreciate that he's a puppy and excited. Just don't start getting all New Agey on me."

Hunt huffed. "You're such a cynic."

"I might be a cynic, but I'm a happy cynic. Happy that you actually came by to see me. I was beginning to think you were only capable of migrating from your Bat Cave to your mother's stately mansion. What a relief to know you still remember how to drive out here! See, I can be as enthusiastic as that dog of yours. Speaking of which, go bring him down from upstairs." Fred had taken a sudden detour and veered to the right in the upstairs hallway.

Hunt trudged up the stairs, frowning when he had to grip the handrail for leverage. He hated being weak. More than that he hated having other people see him this way.

Was it any wonder why he had started to avoid people in general? And if he had to go out, that he made a point of putting up a good front, especially with his mother? His mother… For all her outward concern, she was supremely intolerant of sickness. He knew she thought it a sign of weakness. "I simply refuse to be sick," she was fond of announcing to him in particular.

It was easy to think that way, Hunt surmised, when you've never been sick a day in your life, not that he'd ever pointed that out. Not that she would have listened.

By the time he reached the top of the stairs, Hunt was puffing. He stopped to regain his breath, then whistled. No response. "Fred, where are you, buddy?" He pulled the dog's leash from his back pocket.

From downstairs, Ben's footsteps moved away from the stairs. "I've got to clean up the living room before this baby shower, and I don't want to find out that he's gotten into something up there," he called up.

A moment later Hunt descended with Fred on the leash. He found Ben in the study. "I hope you weren't too attached to that particular roll of toilet paper. I found another one in the vanity and hid the shredded bits in there instead."

Ben finished straightening up the piles of library books and magazines. "Good. A move like that will make Katarina think that Matt did it," he said, referring to his son.

To give Ben due credit, Matt, besides toting the usual baggage of a sixteen-year-old, had only recently come into his life after the death of his mother. Neither Ben nor Matt had known about each other before the reading of the will, and while both were determined to make the relationship work, they were still feeling their way. Katarina helped with smoothing out the relationship, providing mediation and the love, and a secret weapon— her grandmother.

"I don't think the kid has anything to worry about," Hunt replied to Ben. "Hey, the kid can take care of himself. After all, he'd have Lena defending him like a mother hen no matter what."

Ben hunted around for a place to put a pile of old

newspapers and settled for dumping it in the log carrier by the fireplace. "That oughta do it. Amada is away for the week visiting her cousin in Mexico, and I was put in charge of tidying up. You don't know how to vacuum, do you?"

"How hard can it be? If I can graduate from Grantham University, I should be able to work a simple machine. Here, hold the dog, and point the way."

"It's in the hall closet." Ben took Fred's leash. The dog eyed him cautiously, then pulled away with all his might in the direction of Hunt. "I don't think Fred has quite warmed up to me."

Hunt came back dragging the canister vacuum behind him. "Don't take it personally. He's afraid of men. Try looking smaller." Hunt bent down and peered around the back of the vacuum. "There must be a cord hiding somewhere."

Ben hunched his shoulders, but at six foot three it was a little hard to look small. Then he tried sitting on the arm of the couch. Fred just pulled harder. "I don't think this is working." He nodded toward Hunt. "It's down on the left side."

"Check." Hunt pulled out a length of cord and plugged it in.

"So if he's afraid of men, why is he so fond of you? Oh, I forgot, it's your naturally unthreatening charm."

"What's that?" The sound of the vacuum cleaner filled the small space.

"I was just commenting on your wimpiness," Ben shouted.

"You can't rile me," Hunt yelled back. "I'm perfectly secure in my manhood. Witness my confident manner with the vacuum cleaner." He pushed it toward Ben and

caught the ragged edge of an ancient Oriental rug, causing the machine to grab. The noise changed to a desperate high-pitched gurgle, like blackbirds swarming in an
air-conditioning vent.

Fred jumped back, cowering behind Ben's leg.

Hunt tried pulling the vacuum away, but that only
made the machine grip harder.

"Turn the damn thing off," Ben shouted.

"What?"

Ben stood up and stepped on the power button. "I
said," he still shouted before realizing it wasn't necessary. "Sorry," he lowered his voice.

Fred inched forward and bravely inspected the
vacuum. There was a faint burning smell.

Hunt crouched down and worked the rug free from
the bottom of the vacuum.

Fred nudged his thigh.

"It's okay, boy." He fondled the dog's ear.

The puppy lifted a hind leg and scratched at his belly.
The three paws remaining on the wood floor immediately splayed out from under him. His belly plopped
on the floor. He looked up at Hunt and over to Ben,
seemingly proud, as if that was what he meant to do all
along.

Hunt laughed. Fred was good for making him laugh.
Not much else did these days. Then he stood and looked
forlornly at the vacuum. "Well, if I proved one thing, it's
that even though my virility may be intact, I'm nowhere
near as competent as the average woman."

As soon as he'd said the words, Hunt felt the stir-
rings in his libido. Until he caught sight of his water
aerobics partner he wasn't all that convinced that his
loss of sexual desire was a temporary side effect of his

chemo as his oncologist had assured him. *But, aah, the miracle of a teeny-tiny electric-orange bikini,* he thought with a smile.

"Now that we've got that straight, I declare the job done," Ben announced. He passed the dog's leash to Hunt and unplugged the vacuum. "So, tell me, how did that aerobics class go?"

Hunt blinked. Had his friend been reading his mind?

"I know I kind of backed you into it, and for once, I was actually feeling a bit guilty." Ben searched around the end of the vacuum, trying to figure out how to push the cord back in its hole. Brute force didn't appear to be the answer. "Did it work out okay?"

"Well, it was wet and completely embarrassing, so I hope that makes you feel even more guilty."

"So who did they match you up with then?" Ben glanced up. "There must be some way to push the cord back in, don't you think?"

"You knew about the whole partner bit?"

"I suppose I might as well come clean. I wasn't sure you'd go through with it if you knew it required close personal contact with a stranger. So who was it? Some old man recovering from angioplasty?"

"No, actually it was a woman, about thirty maybe."

Ben dropped the cord, raised his hands and stood up. "I'm done." He faced Hunt. "So what was she recovering from?"

Hunt frowned. "I'd say *recovery* is not quite the right word."

Fred tiptoed tentatively toward the vacuum. He put his nose down by the exhaust and sniffed.

Ben frowned. "What do you mean?"

"She's pregnant, bro."

"Pregnant? So where's the father?"

Fred slumped down on his belly and began gnawing on a corner of the plastic casing.

"Apparently not in the picture." Hunt stared off, not focusing on anything in particular. "What is it about fathers and their children, anyway?"

Ben growled.

Hunt quickly explained. "No, man. You didn't even know that Matt existed until last year. I was just commenting on the sorry state of affairs in general. I mean, you never even knew *your* father. Mine barely acknowledged my existence. My most vivid memory of him is not his face, but this big black Cadillac driving away. When he died while I was still young, I realized I didn't miss my father, but that shiny limousine was another matter."

"If it will make you feel any better, I'll buy you a set of whitewalls on eBay," Ben said.

Hunt smiled. "Spoken like a true friend and, I must admit, a good father."

"Tell that to Matt."

"No, Matt knows you'll always be there for him," Hunt said. *The way you were always there for me through cancer,* Hunt could have said, but being a guy, he didn't. When it came down to it, he really wasn't New Agey after all, just his stiff-upper-lip mother's son.

"So what's with this woman's husband then? How come he's not there doing squat thrusts or jumping jacks or whatever it is you do in the shallow end?"

"Some of us have already chosen to do underwater jogging in the deep end with floaties."

"Floaties?"

"A technical term. I'll enlighten you later," Hunt said. "Anyway, as to the lady in question, my partner—" the term sounded strange but surprisingly not unwelcome "—from what she said, I'm not sure if there was ever one on the scene."

Ben whistled. "An unwed mother, huh?"

"Single parent is the politically correct term these days," Hunt corrected.

Fred turned his head and mouthed furiously on a button along the bottom edge by the left rear wheel.

"There didn't have to be a guy, you know. It could have been a sperm bank donor," Ben suggested hypothetically.

"Who knows? She made it pretty clear she wasn't into men," Hunt replied.

"She's gay?" Ben asked.

"She didn't say that, and I didn't ask."

Fred bit down, and the cord suddenly sprang into action, retracting on command. It snaked in quickly and the plug smacked Fred in the butt. The dog seemed stunned, then gave a delayed bark.

Ben shook his head. "How do you like that? We're actually stupider than that dumb dog of yours. Forget your average female." He made a face back at Hunt. "So, was she okay to look at?"

Hunt watched Fred lick his fur. He exhaled. "To tell you the truth, it wouldn't have mattered if she were only attracted to hedgehogs. And the fact that she's pregnant? Weird maybe, but *so* not a problem. It just made her all the more womanly. In fact, everything about her turned me on."

CHAPTER SIX

AFTER SARAH'S SPEEDY RECOVERY, the three pedicures, and, luckily, no further dramas, Julie drove them all to Katarina's. She pulled into the driveway, and Katarina glanced over her shoulder to the backseat of the Honda CR-V. "She's asleep. Is that a bad sign?"

Julie turned off the engine. "I think it's perfectly normal for a woman in her thirtieth week of pregnancy to fall asleep at the end of a long day. It's other things that have me concerned," she said in a low voice. She glanced behind, then pointed outside, out of earshot.

Katarina nodded and, wincing as she opened the door as quietly as possible, tiptoed out. They huddled together by the driver's-side headlight, their backs to the car.

Katarina began, "I thought you said that dizziness happened occasionally when you're pregnant, especially if the mom-to-be is overheated or hasn't eaten in a while."

Julie shook her head. "I know what I said. That Sarah was sitting down, allowing the blood to collect in her lower limbs, and when she stood up, not enough blood returned to her heart and her blood pressure dropped, causing her to faint. That part's simple."

"Are you worried about something else?"

"She comes in every two weeks at this stage, but I'd

like to see her sooner. I don't think it's something more serious, but I don't want to take any chances."

"So there's no need to worry then, right?"

"Wrong. There's every chance in the world that her fainting could happen again."

"But if she takes precautions—you mentioned getting up slowly, lying on her side instead of her back, eating a bunch of small meals."

"That will help, but what if she faints while she's driving? What then?"

Katarina covered her mouth with her hand. "Oh, my God. That could be serious."

A noise came from the car.

They turned around guiltily.

Sarah stood by the open door of the backseat. She was holding on to the edge of the door, appearing none too steady on her feet.

Katarina moved quickly. "Hey, kiddo, how are you feeling? You were out for the count, so we thought we'd let you sleep some more in the car."

"Good thinking." Sarah tried to look at her feet and frowned. She was still wearing flip-flops after having her pedicure, with a long piece of tissue woven between her toes to keep the polish from smudging. That's right, her shoes were in her small nylon knapsack. She turned around to find them, wobbling a little. "Maybe I'm not quite up for this baby-shower thing."

Julie came over by her side. "Don't worry. No one should be here for another half hour or more. Besides, it's not like it's such a big deal. We just invited a few people to make it festive. Rosemary from work and some of your clients and neighbors."

Katarina circled around Sarah and lifted the knapsack

off the backseat. "Here, let me get your stuff. Julie can get my bag along with hers."

"At least let me carry the pie. I'm not a complete invalid, you know," Sarah insisted. She took a few steps along the gravel drive and felt a bit dizzy again. Maybe carrying the pie wasn't smart after all. She stopped and breathed in slowly. No, she could do this. A question of mind over matter.

She stared straight ahead and squared her shoulders. It wasn't more than ten feet into Katarina's house, even if she did have to step around a sexy black Porsche that blocked the direct route.

Julie ran her fingers over the sleek fender. "Has Ben traded in his motorcycle for this little beauty?" she asked.

"Uh, no…" Katarina replied. "It's—"

Sarah didn't bother to wait for Katarina since she knew the back door to the house was always unlocked. Grantham was preternaturally safe by the world's standards. Anyway, Katarina had once explained that if any thief could possibly find their little stone cottage off a hidden country road that snaked along the canal, let alone make his way up their long, dark driveway, she would personally direct him to Ben's supply of fly-fishing paraphernalia. She had been trying to clean the mess up for months to no avail.

So, without waiting, Sarah turned the knob and with accustomed familiarity stepped into the kitchen and placed the pie on the countertop by the sink.

She had barely turned to make way for the others when she heard a frantic scurrying.

Pounce!

Whoosh! The air went out of her lungs.

Twice in one day, Sarah hit the deck, though this time safely on her rump. Even with extra padding the terracotta tiles hit hard.

But they were nothing compared to the two paws pressed on her shoulder blades. Or the wet tongue attacking her nose.

She winced and tried to turn away.

The dog lavished a kiss on her ear, and Sarah couldn't help but laugh. "So, don't tell me. Is this a surprise guest?" She grabbed on to Fred's neck as he continued to slobber her cheeks and nose. "Is it my imagination or is this dog seriously excited. I mean, take a look down there." She couldn't stop laughing.

"Sarah!" Katarina shouted. She stormed across the kitchen. "Are you okay? Ben what's going on here?"

Julie stripped off her coat and draped it across one of the wooden chairs around the kitchen table. She crossed her arms. "Here—" she stepped toward Sarah "—let me pull him off you."

At the sound of Julie's words, the dog collapsed directly on Sarah's chest. "Easier said than done," Sarah said. At a loss for a better solution, she lay down on the hard tiles, and the dog went with her. His back legs spread-eagled, his body forming a convex shroud over Sarah's ballooning stomach. He rested his snout between Sarah's breasts, his wet nose burrowing against the hollow between her collarbone. "It's always nice to be wanted," she said good-naturedly.

Katarina stomped down the hallway. "Ben! I know you're here somewhere!"

Sarah heard the sound of footsteps approaching the kitchen and expected to hear some major groveling from

Ben. *This should be good,* she thought, and angled her neck to deprive the dog of a clear shot at her mouth.

Only it wasn't Ben.

First, she saw long legs in loose-fitting chinos that creased informally around a pair of well-worn boat shoes. She angled her chin up and got an upside-down view. Of a blondish man with wire-rimmed glasses and wearing a baggy crewneck sweater that looked like one of those old L.L.Bean black-and-white Norwegian numbers. From this perspective, she couldn't get a really good look at his face, but she could see plainly that the sweater was raveling at the cuffs and had a patch on one elbow.

First impressions might indicate someone down on his luck, but Sarah knew better. She had lived in Grantham long enough to recognize the trappings of Old Money. Except for a few of her physical therapy clients, she didn't mix with the old guard. Not that they weren't unfailingly polite. It's just that invitations to join the exclusive tennis club on the west side of town, where the clay courts were always immaculately groomed and white tennis clothes were mandatory, had never reached her—not that she could have afforded it or particularly yearned for it.

But the weird thing was, his legs had a certain familiarity to them. Sarah squinted and shifted the dog to get her shoulders around and get a more upright view. And then it hit her.

"Fred, buddy, I know you're a ladies' man, but do you think you could be a little more subtle about it?" He bent over and grabbed the dog by his collar and lifted him off Sarah. He roughed up the fur around his collar even as the dog danced about his feet. "It's okay, calm down. Sit."

If anything the dog pranced more.

He pushed its rump down with his hand and the dog finally sat, his tail still wagging in double-time.

Still petting the dog, he spoke without looking over. "I'm sorry about that. He's usually afraid of strangers, but it seems you made a rather large impression on him." He looked up.

"Hunt? You're Hunt, right?" Sarah asked with surprise. Only now did she again see how hollow the flesh was beneath his jutting cheekbones.

"Sarah?" he asked, equally startled. He rubbed his hand over the dog's back involuntarily. "You're here for the party? Katarina's party? I never expected…"

The two of them stared dumbfounded at each other, unaware of the others in the kitchen.

"You look different," he said finally. "You're not wearing a bathing suit."

"And you're wearing glasses," she said.

Julie stepped next to Sarah. "Am I missing something here?"

Katarina marched back into the kitchen with Ben in tow. "Would someone mind filling me in here?" she asked.

Sarah twisted toward one friend then the other. She levered her weight on one hand, ready to hoist herself up.

Everyone rushed to help. Hunt was first. Hunt and Fred. He—Hunt, not Fred—placed his hand under her upper arm and guided her up like a tugboat maneuvering a cruise ship. He didn't let go when she was finally standing.

Sarah gulped. An awkward moment or two passed. "I think I can stand on my own now."

"Oh, right." Hunt stepped back. He seemed momentarily startled, too, but recovered after a beat to say, "And to think we coordinated all that after only one water aerobics lesson. Imagine if we'd had two?"

Sarah drank in his easy grin. "Yes, just imagine," she said haltingly.

And she could, only too well.

CHAPTER SEVEN

KATARINA HONED IN ON HIM, Hunt backed away, only
to run up against the kitchen counter.

"You have the nerve to turn me down?" She was
aghast.

"It's not that, and I really appreciate the invitation.
It's just that…ah…I think it would probably be better
if I…ah…I didn't stay. I mean, besides, what do I know
about baby showers?" Except that the usual decorum
probably didn't involve one of the guests harboring lust-
ful thoughts every time he saw the mother-to-be. Hunt
cleared his throat. "Then there's Fred. He's not really
comfortable around strangers." He looked down at his
dog who chose that second to wag his tail and appear
particularly cute.

Katarina smiled at the dog, which didn't stop her
from poking Hunt in the chest. "I can't believe it. A
grown man hiding behind a thirty-pound dog."

"He's more like thirty-five."

"Please, you'll have to do better than that. Anyway,
Matt's back from orchestra practice at the high school,
and he volunteered to look after Frodo or whatever he's
called.

"Fred."

"Fred? What kind of a name is that for a dog?"

Julie sauntered into the kitchen.

Hunt eyed her nervously before responding to Sarah. "There's nothing wrong with Fred. Many outstanding individuals have been named Fred. Frederick Douglass. Fred Astaire."

"Fred Flintstone," Julie added. She opened the refrigerator door. "Hey, you got any half-and-half in here? I want to fill the creamer for the coffee."

Katarina glanced over but she didn't budge. Hunt was still wedged against the edge of the counter. "You'll have to use the two-percent milk. I'm watching Ben's cholesterol."

Julie grabbed the half-gallon jug and straightened up. She sauntered over in her bare feet, her newly polished dusky-rose toenails a bright splash of color against the dark Mexican tile floor. She pressed her chin forward and, using all her six-foot-two height, greeted Hunt eyeball to eyeball. "Long time no see, Hunt. But then you probably don't remember me from GHS," she said, referring to Grantham High School. "Julie? Julie Antonelli? You were a year ahead of me."

"And you were always an inch taller," he answered back.

She gave Hunt a withering stare. "Not only does he have to stay, I say we make him demonstrate the pass-the-orange-under-your-chin-without-using-your-hands game." She flipped her bangs imperiously, pivoted on her heels and made her way out of the kitchen, holding the milk aloft.

Hunt watched her go with an exhalation of relief. "Even in school she was always this scary."

"You're lucky. You've caught her on a good day. So what do you say? Now that you're here…"

Hunt looked up at the ceiling. Heavy wooden beams,

darkened with age, ran crosswise across the room. They cleared only a few inches above his head. He shifted his gaze back to Katarina. "You don't have to include me just because I happened to be on the premises. I don't know the first thing about baby showers."

"Not important. Besides, I'm far too uncoordinated to demonstrate the party game, and Julie's already turned me down cold." Katarina looked at him beseechingly.

"Okay." He caved. "But only because I happen to like you so much."

Katarina laughed and gave him a peck on the cheek and let go of his arm. "How about you take down the white dessert plates from the overhead cupboard behind you and put them on the dining room table, to the left of the silverware?"

"If I get the coffee cups, too, can I forgo this orange-whatever thing?" He turned around.

"No, but nice try," she said behind his back and added in an oh-so-casual tone, "So you and Sarah already know each other then? From the adult education class? You know, I still can't believe you're doing water aerobics."

Hunt grabbed the plates and turned back. "You mean Ben didn't tell you how he practically strong-armed me?"

Katarina let her tongue rest on her top lip. "Oh, right. Ben."

Hunt looked at her askance. The corner of his mouth twitched up in amusement. "He didn't tell you a thing, did he?"

Katarina held up her index finger. "No, but I'm prepared to get to the bottom of it." She leaned toward the hallway. "Hey, Sarah, could you come in here a sec?" she shouted. She crossed her arms and waited.

Sarah waddled into the room, her flip-flops slapping the floor. "You need something?"

"Just some clarification. Did you know that Ben pushed Hunt into taking the water aerobics class?"

Sarah rubbed her chin as she thought. "At the pool he mentioned something about friends signing him up, but no real details."

Katarina narrowed her eyes. "The plot thickens."

From outside, the sound of a car engine signaled Ben's return from the caterer's.

Katarina opened the door and didn't waste any time while he carried in the parcels of prepared food. "So, when did you get the idea of having Hunt take the class?" she asked, barely letting him put the overflowing shopping bags on the table.

"I don't know. It just kind of hit me, the wisdom of the whole 'education as the wellspring of life' thing," Ben said. He waved sheepishly to Hunt and Sarah.

Hunt stepped toward his best buddy. "Nice try, but I'm afraid not entirely believable. Listen, it's no use trying to save face." Hunt appealed to Katarina. "Don't give him a hard time. Ben already confessed to me that he fell prey to a force far greater than he—my mother. She was the one who put him up to it."

Ben sighed. "I admit it. I was beaten down. It *was* Iris's idea."

"I still don't know what that has to do with me," Sarah protested. "After all, *my* clients gave me the gift certificate for the class."

Hunt turned to her. "And who are your clients?"

"Well, let's see. Wanda and Rufus, and oh right, Lena."

"*Babička!*" Katarina exclaimed, using the Slovak word for *grandmother.*

"You don't think that your grandmother?" Sarah blinked at Katarina.

"And my mother?" Hunt added.

Katarina beamed. "Conspired to set you two up? You betcha."

"Well, that's just absurd," Sarah protested.

"Even if they did, it's irrelevant. After all, we're both adults. We're perfectly capable of forming our own personal relationships without outside interference," Hunt said emphatically.

"Ya think?" Katarina viewed them both skeptically. Then she turned to Ben. "Come, my strong husband. How about you and I bring the food into the dining room? I've already got platters waiting on the table." She motioned toward the shopping bags, and he picked them up, cradling the heavy packages in both arms, and followed her out of the kitchen.

Hunt watched his friend shuffle out dutifully. "Oh, how the mighty have fallen."

"On the contrary, I'd say theirs is a relationship based on mutual understanding," Sarah responded. She cocked her head, her mouth open, as if waiting for him to disagree.

Hunt paused, considering a witty comeback, but no easy retort came to mind. Instead, he found his attention straying to her parted lips.

Sarah nervously dropped her eyes. "Not that *I* want or particularly need something along those lines myself right now."

Hunt gathered himself. "Of course not. Nor I," he said emphatically.

"So we're just going to forget about this little match-making stunt, correct?" she asked, raising her head.

"Absolutely. Consider it forgotten," he proclaimed.

But, in truth, he wasn't sure he really could. Especially when he noticed the way a little vertical line formed between her brows when she frowned so earnestly. he felt his fingers itch with the impulse to smooth it flat.

"So," he said in a forced upbeat tone, "should we rejoin the fray?"

She seemed to hesitate, then nodded.

"Just one thing?" He didn't want to release her quite yet.

"Yes?" The crease deepened.

He knew he was a goner. "When they call for volunteers to help me demonstrate this party game? Under no circumstances accept."

CHAPTER EIGHT

"So you're a surprise," Sarah said, sitting on the couch in the living room. She slipped off a flip-flop as she wiggled a foot into one of the sneakers she had liberated from her knapsack. She grunted. Pretty soon she was going to have to give up tie shoes, she realized. Already half her shoes no longer fit her swollen feet.

"Well, I aim to please," Hunt said. He had put dessert dishes on the dining room table, careful to avoid any direct conversation with Julie who was doing something mysterious with the paper napkins. "Here, let me do that."

He circled the couch and sat on the edge of the coffee table. Behind him, logs crackled in the fireplace, taking the chill off the early fall air. He reached for the sneaker and caught hold of her foot with the other hand. "Jeez, your feet are cold." Seemingly without thinking, Hunt dropped the shoe and started rubbing her toes. He couldn't help it. It was too much of a temptation.

"I think this is my cue to leave," Julie said loudly.

"No need," Sarah protested over her shoulder, but Julie had already left the room. "Oh, well." She looked down and would have felt embarrassed except it felt so good.

"So when are you due?"

"Hmm?" Sarah was lost in the feeling of his hands working the balls of her feet.

"I said when are you due? That's the correct thing to ask at a baby shower, I presume."

Sarah shook her head. That's right. She still had a baby shower to face. "Ten weeks," she said. "Give or take."

"So you must be pretty excited? Got the baby stuff already?"

"Not really. I mean, I've already checked out IKEA online, and know exactly what I want, but I've kind of put off driving up to Newark and actually buying everything."

He looked at her protruding belly. "I'm not sure putting off anything is the best course of action at this point."

"Ya think?" she said with a laugh.

"So at least you're not putting off this baby shower?"

"Did I have any choice? Not with friends like Katarina and Julie organizing it."

"Katarina is a cupcake, but that Julie…I don't know about her."

"No, no, she's great, really. We work together at the hospital, and believe me, she practically bleeds for her patients."

"You're nurses?" Hunt seemed to immediately realize his mistake. "Sorry, male chauvinist assumption. You're doctors?"

"Julie's an obstetrician. I'm a physical therapist."

"Cool. And I really mean that. You're actually helping people, something I wish I could say. In fact, I've been thinking about that a lot." He reflected a moment more. "But enough about me. Hey, since you're the expert, you should be rubbing *my* feet." He looked in her sports bag. "No socks?"

"No, I'm a little behind with the wash. I can't seem to get on top of things these days. And now with the water aerobics class…"

"Tell me about it." He slipped the one shoe on and tied the laces tightly and efficiently.

Sarah looked down. "You're very good at that. You could probably have an alternate career as a foot masseur if you wanted, and you'd definitely be helping out womenkind."

Hunt slipped off the other flip-flop. "I like your nail polish," he said before pushing up the bridge of his wire-rimmed glasses and starting his magic on her other foot. "It matches your bathing suit."

"That's what I thought, too." She stared at his hands. They had long fingers, pianist hands. Mesmerized, she watched while he manipulated her instep. It was so sublime, almost an out-of-body experience. "So if I'm in denial about having a baby, what are you hiding from?" she asked.

Hunt concentrated on gently rotating her heel. "Well, I suppose the most obvious thing would be having had cancer."

"I figured you had." Sarah straightened her neck. "You've been through chemo recently?"

He rested her foot on his thigh and found her other sneaker in her bag.

When he didn't reply right away, she shook her head. "I'm sorry. I didn't mean to pry if you don't want to talk about it. I mean, it's really none of my business."

He adjusted his glasses again, even though they appeared perfectly straight. "No, it's all right. It's just that most people avoid the subject."

"They probably are afraid of hurting you."

He raised his head and looked at her squarely. "Frankly, I think it's more like they're afraid of hurting themselves."

Sarah frowned.

"Deep down I think they're afraid it might be contagious, that they might get it, too."

"That's just nuts!"

"I know it's not logical, but people get a little touchy when they start thinking about their own mortality."

Sarah instinctively rubbed her tummy. She cocked her head. "So does it help to talk about it? Your condition?"

"Why don't we find out? And if it makes you feel better, I could act all noble."

"Excuse me, I'm not the one who needs to feel better, but if you really want, you could rub that foot some more. This excess water weight is a bitch."

Hunt smiled and rested her sneaker on the couch and worked on her arch some more.

"Ah, you are a god." She closed her eyes. "So what kind of cancer, anyway?"

"Lymphoma," he said.

She opened her eyes. "And you found out because…?"

He ran his tongue along his chapped lips. "I noticed a swollen lymph node in my neck, and this feeling of being tired that wouldn't go away. I first went to my internist, who referred me to an oncologist in the city. That was that. Stage I Hodgkin's lymphoma, the cancer that tends to strike young…or, well…youngish men. Fortunately, patients have a surprisingly high rate of survival, especially when the disease is caught early."

"Is this where I'm supposed to say you must have been overjoyed with the news?"

"Absolutely!" he said emphatically.

She looked at him askance. "I thought we said no nobility."

Hunt stilled his hand on the top of Sarah's foot. "Okay, the truth is that you go through these reactions—denial, anger, bargaining, depression and finally acceptance. The whole grieving process."

"And now you've gone through all the stages?" she asked.

"What's today?" He reached for her sneaker.

"Thursday," she answered.

"Ask me tomorrow," he said, and slipped the shoe on.

"And tomorrow?" she asked again.

"Ask me next week." He tied the laces and swung her leg off his.

"And in the meantime?"

"I'll just have to—"

She waved him off before he could finish. "I know, I know. You'll just have to act noble." She paused. "And the chemo?"

"ABVD," he said, referring to the cocktail of drugs. "Every two weeks for six months."

"But you're done now, right?"

"Three months. Three clean months."

"Which is great! I mean, that sounds great. But maybe I should ask you tomorrow or the next week, right?"

IN THOSE FEW WORDS, HUNT KNEW that Sarah understood. The feeling that he should be happy, but he just wasn't ready for all that happiness.

Here was this woman whom he didn't really know, who didn't really know him—well, who'd seen him in bathing trunks, which is more than he would let his family and close friends do at the moment, who understood.

And that made him happier than he'd been in a long while, if you didn't count Fred jumping on the bed every morning and licking his face for a "good morning" wake-up call.

But one thing for sure—today, tomorrow or next week—Fred wasn't Sarah. Fred didn't have him fantasizing about gliding together in the lap pool on the roof of his house, and bobbing together shoulder to shoulder, hands on each other's arms, legs…well…her legs wrapped around his waist in ways that could not really be described as isometric…. He could feel the beginning of an arousal, and clearing his throat, casually rested his hand to cover the strain against the inseam of his pants. All this in response to a woman who was pregnant, and not only pregnant—pregnant with another man's baby.

He breathed slowly, and when he felt under control, he turned, quite pleased. "You're right, you know," he said. "You're so very right. *And* you have beautiful toes. So, to celebrate these two lucky events let me say that even though I didn't know about the event ahead of time, I am delighted to be here to celebrate your baby shower."

"Which means you were originally here because…"

"Because I'm a friend of Ben's, and his business partner, too. Anyway, I happened to be here to discuss certain plans, future plans, really—"

There was a loud knock at the front door.

Sarah looked at Hunt. "I'm sorry. It appears that the hordes are descending, which means it's time to put on that happy face." She pushed up the corners of her mouth. Then she wedged her arm behind her and started to push herself up. "Jeez, I didn't know this thing was so squishy," she said when she didn't make much headway.

The rapping on the door sounded again.

"I'll get it. I'll get it." Julie swept in from the study.

"Here, let me help," Hunt said to Sarah. He stood up and hooked a hand under her arm. Sarah grunted and tried to leverage herself. She was halfway up when she put her hand to her head. "Hold it, a sec," she said, and plopped down again.

The sudden movement pulled him forward, and his chest landed on hers.

Which is how Rufus, Sarah's office manager Rosemary, and Julie found them.

"HI, EVERYONE." SARAH LEANED to the side and waved. "Hunt was just helping me get up."

"That's the first thing I thought when I saw you two that way," Rufus said. He smiled, but then Rufus was always smiling, or so Sarah told herself. "Anywhere special I should put this present?" He held up a large wrapped box. "I want to lend a hand and help you get up, too. It looks like fun."

Hunt backed off Sarah and wiped his hands. "Thanks, but I think we'll be able to figure it second go-round. Shall we?" He held out a hand.

Sarah harrumphed and wriggled her butt to get closer to the edge of the couch. "All right. I'm ready for liftoff. Let's do it." With Hunt hoisting her up and providing balance against her back, Sarah tottered into an upright position.

"We've still got more people to go, but things are definitely starting to rumble," Katarina proclaimed as she and Ben joined the group in the living room. Katarina was fussing with her hair, replacing a clip that appeared to have slipped out. Her sensitive redhead skin was flushed.

There was another knock, and Katarina's neighbors and more of Sarah's patients spilled in.

"I wouldn't miss it, especially when I heard that Sarah baked a cherry pie, my favorite. It's enough to make you forget all about cholesterol and HDLs," Sarah's office manager, Rosemary, said. An enamel pin of twin baby shoes adorned her V-neck sweater. She passed her present to Ben and the others did likewise.

Ben looked to Katarina. "Where do you want these?"

"You can put them on the sideboard in the dining room," she said, using her finger to count heads.

Hunt raised his eyebrows at Sarah. "You managed to bake a pie, but you don't have time to wash socks?"

"So maybe my priorities are a little skewed, but you'll think differently after you've eaten some." She turned to welcome the group. "Gosh, I can't believe you all came out on a week night. That's so sweet. Katarina said it would be just a few people, but this is a little overwhelming." Then she blinked. "If we're all here, I say let the party begin."

"Hold on," Katarina said at the sound of another car pulling into the gravel driveway. "I think I hear a few more people. She glanced out the narrow sidelight by the front door. "Sarah, why don't you come by the door and help me greet the remaining stragglers? Everybody else, gather around, too."

Hunt maneuvered next to Ben. "Here, let me help you do the manly thing with the boxes."

Ben dumped them all in Hunt's outstretched arms. "I thought you were confident in your masculinity."

Hunt juggled the boxes. "A real man knows when to build up brownie points."

There was a knock at the door. Louder than the first two had been.

Katarina stepped to the door. "I'd recognize my grandmother's rapping anywhere. Her knuckles are so strong from making all that strudel."

Julie sniffed loudly. "Never mind the strudel. I can smell her plum cake wafting through the door. Now the party can really begin."

Katarina held up her hand. "Not so fast." She swung open the door.

In stepped Lena Zemanova, the aroma from the freshly baked plum cake preceding her. She crossed the threshold, turned around, and made a yanking motion with her head. There was the sound of soft-soled footsteps on the stone front step.

Everyone bent their heads to get a better view.

A polyester pant leg and a single cream-colored FootJoy came into view.

"Surprise!" Lena shouted. She gestured triumphantly with her hand.

"Oh, my God!" Sarah blanched and covered her mouth.

Katarina clapped and gazed proudly at Sarah. "You never guessed, did you?"

Sarah shook her head. Slowly. She had yet to blink

since the door opened. "Everybody, this is my mom, Penny Halverson, all the way from Minnesota."

They all shuffled forward for introductions

Except for Sarah. Instead she wobbled back and forth.

Hunt dropped the boxes.

And caught her in midcrumple.

CHAPTER NINE

"MOM, I STILL CAN'T believe you came." Sarah wiped her cheeks with the back of her hand and sniffed away the tears that wouldn't stop coming. The baby shower had been fun, and everyone seemed to have had a good time and eaten more than their fair share. In fact, once she had gotten a piece of cake herself, the way Julie had reminded her, her dizziness had subsided immediately—much to everyone's relief.

And they were all much too generous.

Now she had all these cute little outfits and a fancy jogging stroller. It was sitting, adorned with a large bow, in front of the fireplace in Katarina and Ben's living room, while Sarah and her mother reclined on the couch. This time, Sarah had thought to put a throw pillow behind her back so getting up wouldn't require the jaws of life.

Just about all the guests had gone except for Julie and Lena and her mother of course. And Rufus. He, Hunt and Ben had mysteriously disappeared into the study.

"As if I wouldn't come to my only daughter's baby shower! I can't tell you how delighted I was to get Katarina's call," Penny said. "And you know, your pie was delicious. You must give me the recipe."

"It's Aunt Gladys's, Mom. I know your apple-rhubarb

pie has won blue ribbons, but Aunt Gladys's cherry pie is pretty good, too."

"You are so right. At the church auctions, her cherry pie always went first. Tell me, what's that flavoring in her crust?"

"Nutmeg."

Penny nodded. "I knew it. Gladys would never tell me. She's so competitive, a typical oldest child. She always had to be best—at school, with beaux, even what parts she got in the Christmas pageant. Somehow she never did get used to having to share Mother's affection when the rest of us came along." She looked at the flames flickering in the fireplace. "Nutmeg, you say?"

Sarah nodded philosophically. "How come families are always so complicated? Nothing ever seems to just run smoothly like in books or on TV. You and Aunt Gladys always on edge. Wayne, losing his job at the printing factory in Duluth last year." Wayne was her second brother who had moved back in with their parents.

"Well, it's not like he sat on his duff. You know he found a job at the local Home Depot, don't you?"

"Yeah, I suppose that's something to be grateful for. But what about other things like Dad having to get two stents. Thank God, he gave up smoking."

"And didn't I hear about it." Penny *tsked*. "Now I have to listen to him going on about how the doctors don't let him eat anything with taste to it. You know he's banned low-fat yogurt from the house?"

Sarah wiped another tear from her cheek. "Yeah, that would be Dad. I don't know how you put up with it."

Penny patted her on the thigh. "Listen, no matter

what, we just about all manage to come together on Thanksgiving, even if Gladys always makes such a fuss." Penny didn't mention that Sarah hadn't made it to many Thanksgivings in the past ten years or so.

Still, she could easily imagine her father rising from the table after polishing off two helpings of tofu pumpkin pie. He'd pull the waistband of his trousers up over his belly—granted, smaller than it had been in years—and go over and kiss his wife's forehead before retiring to his recliner and football.

There was nothing wrong with her family, Sarah realized, even if this was the rare occasion when conversation didn't end with her gnashing her teeth or feeling as if she'd let them down in myriad ways.

And now she wondered, as she fingered the fine stitching on the baby quilt that her mother had given her, had she ever succeeded in her quest to transform herself into something more—something more interesting? After all, here she was happily sharing baking secrets with her mother. Talk about predictable. But was predictable necessarily wrong?

She scrunched the quilt to her face and breathed in the fresh scent from drying on a clothesline. "I know I thanked you already, Mom, but I can't begin to tell you how much it means to me that you brought me the family quilt," she said from the heart.

Penny chuckled. "Why of course, silly girl. It's always been passed down from mother to daughter. That's the tradition in our family. I can't tell you how long I've been waiting for this moment." Penny beamed and patted her daughter on her knee.

That only set off another bout of tears.

"Sorry. It's just the hormones." But Sarah knew it was

more. "Oh, Mom—" she hiccupped "—I know you say it's a family tradition, but I'm hardly leading my life in a very traditional way. I haven't exactly embraced the married couple, nuclear family model."

Penny frowned thoughtfully. "No but…"

The sound of footsteps clumping down the stairs muffled the rest of her words.

"So is it safe to come down yet?" It was Matt, Ben's sixteen-year-old son. He peeked his head into the living room and saw Sarah and her mom. "Sorry, I thought I heard everybody leave, and I was hoping there'd be some leftovers. There's nothing like writing up a chemistry lab to make you hungry. And don't worry. I left the crazy dog in my bedroom."

Sarah laughed and waved hello. She made the introductions to her mother, and Matt made a mumbling attempt at salutations, which Penny seemed to find perfectly normal.

"I think your dad is hiding with Hunt and maybe Rufus in the study. Katarina's with *Babička* in the kitchen, most likely cleaning up," Sarah said. "Julie's with them, so you'll have to fight her for the leftovers."

Matt nodded, his long, skinny neck undulating.

"Okay, I'll even risk *Babička* putting me on cleanup duty just to get a piece of her plum cake." Matt's nose seemed to guide him in the direction of the food, and the sound of laughter and voices could be heard greeting him from the back of the house.

Sarah smiled one moment, but got a little down the next. She sighed. "You know, Mom, I've never considered changing my mind about the baby, but sometimes I wonder if I'm being fair. To the baby. I mean, here I'm going to bring him up alone. He'll only have me to greet him when he comes home from school or play ball with or read stories to him."

She narrowed her eyes and blocked out the crackle of the fireplace and the hum of the oil burner. Instead she focused on the voices and the sound of cabinets and drawers being opened from the kitchen. *That's what home was all about, right?*

Penny turned to her daughter. "How many children with two parents are really happy? Look at all those parents who hire nannies to push their toddlers in swings or enroll them in organized sports from the time they can walk rather than just sit out on the lawn and feel the grass, and look for bugs or watch the clouds float by. You'll do that, Sarah. You were always a great cloud watcher."

Penny's words brought Sarah back to the room. "That's really sweet, Mom. Thanks."

Penny ran her hand over the quilt on her daughter's lap. "You know, I remember you used to insist on carrying around the quilt before you went off to school. Whenever you got tired, you'd just lie down on the sidewalk or on the grass and curl up with your 'quiltie.' That's what you called it. Quiltie."

Sarah examined the quilt more closely. "I remember. Gee, I'm surprised after all that wear and tear that it's in such good shape."

"Well, as soon as I heard about the baby back in June—" Penny tactfully left out the whole wedding fiasco, Sarah noticed "—I got to work repairing it."

"Aw, Mom." Sarah leaned over and rested her head on her mother's shoulder.

Penny leaned her cheek against her daughter's hair.

She sniffed. "It was well worth it. I'm sure your child will love it, too."

"Well, I'll be sure to take good care of—"

In an instant, a whirlwind darted into the living room. Fred. All four paws went in different directions as he raced around the coffee table, two times clockwise and once counterclockwise, ending with a Baryshnikov leap over the table. He landed with his front paws on Sarah.

"Not again," Sarah moaned. She tried to snatch the quilt from under his paws. That only seemed to make Fred more excited as he nervously sniffed it, his head and tail twitching together.

"Off!" Sarah commanded.

Those stern words resulted in Fred kissing her and for good measure, leaning across and kissing Penny.

"Isn't he the darnedest fellow," Penny cooed. "I could just eat him up." She scratched him behind one floppy ear.

Sarah shook her head. "I think it's more like he wants to eat you up, then me, and anything else within easy reach." She arched her neck back and shouted toward the kitchen. "Katarina! We need you! Quick!"

Katarina rushed in with a dishcloth in her hands. "What's wrong? Do you need Julie?" she said, clearly assuming a medical emergency.

Fred wiggled up on the couch between Sarah and Penny, squashing his butt securely against Sarah. He maneuvered his head around and gave her a large slobbering kiss on her ear before lifting his head over the back of the couch to acknowledge Katarina's presence. All in all, he looked pleased to have managed to round up even more playmates.

"Hunt!" Katarina shouted to the study. "Come get your dog. He's attacking Sarah again."

Hunt rushed through the living room doorway, with Ben and Rufus not far behind. "I thought Matt was watching him," he said by way of an apology.

Matt and *Babička* came to see what was going on as well. Matt finished chewing and swallowed. "What the he—"

Babička gave him a stern look.

"I left him upstairs, I swear," he said. "And I closed the door tight."

Julie came out carrying a glass of red wine. "Well, I'm glad it's not a medical emergency because I've had several drinks."

Katarina glared at Hunt as he crossed in front to retrieve Fred. "Excuse me, last I heard, he's your dog, so don't blame it on Matt. The poor kid barely has time to eat, and it's not his fault that that dog of yours seems to be a Houdini at escaping."

"Okay, okay, I get the message." Hunt leaned over and grabbed Fred at the neck. "C'mon, boy."

Fred squirmed and slipped his narrow head out of his webbed collar. He hopped off the couch and scurried between Hunt's legs and began his random chase around the room again.

"Get him," Katarina shouted.

Fred feinted and bobbed away when anyone came near, finally coming to rest near the front door. His long pink tongue hung down to his theoretical shoe laces while he panted. Despite the momentary exhaustion, he still had enough energy to wag his tail.

Penny laughed. "Oh, my, I think he could keep this up for hours. That's a puppy for you."

"That's a pain in the butt for you," Ben qualified. "You should see what he did to Iris's garden."

Babička pressed her hand to her knitted cardigan. "Not her garden! Her place is on the House and Garden Tour this year for the hospital fundraiser. She must be beside herself!"

Rufus stepped toward Katarina. "You wouldn't have any cheese left, would you?"

She nodded.

Rufus signaled to Matt. "Matt, why don't you bring me in a couple of pieces? And, Hunt, I'll take that collar, and if you have a leash, I think I have a solution," Rufus said in his usual placid tones. You would have thought he was shooting the breeze with one of the patrons at his jazz bar.

"Hey, whatever works." Hunt handed the collar to Rufus and retrieved the leash from the study.

Rufus took it and looked up as Matt came back into the room. "Good, I'm armed now." He slowly approached the dog, but rather than loom over him, he went to crouch down. "Whoops, maybe I shouldn't do that. The physical therapy with Sarah has helped a lot, but not enough for this."

Sarah leveraged herself up. "Somebody get Rufus a chair."

Ben got one from the dining room.

"Thanks, put it there." Rufus nodded to the hallway about three feet from the front door. Fred watched intently.

Rufus sat and made a big show of breaking up the cheese into pieces. Fred lowered his head and kept his eyes peeled.

"Fred," Rufus said sweetly, as though he was talking to a dear friend. "Fred." He held out a piece of cheese toward the dog. "Fred, good dog."

Fred inched forward.

Rufus sat there as calm as could be, like fishing on a lazy Sunday morning. "Good dog, Fred. What a good dog." He threw a piece of cheese on the rug close to the dog. Fred stretched his neck and gobbled it up. Then Rufus threw another, not quite so close, all the while cooing and saying words of encouragement. Everyone held their breath, watching the dog inch closer to Rufus.

When he was in grabbing distance, Rufus again said, "Fred," but this time he brought his fist to his chest and added, "Fred, sit."

Fred—the very same Fred the Manic Dog and Fred the Out-of-Control Mutt—cocked his ears and stared at Rufus. And then he sat.

Rufus gave Fred some more cheese. "Good dog." He fondled the dog's ear and slipped the collar over his head and attached the leash.

"Our very own Dog Whisperer," Lena exclaimed.

Ben shook his head. "I always knew you were a great man, but who would have thought you had magical powers."

Rufus continued to rub the dog's ears. "It's not magic. It's just dog training 101." He passed the leash to Hunt. "In fact, if you'd like to learn more, I recommend you sign up for my beginner's obedience class for dogs at the Adult School on Sunday afternoon. I believe there're still a few spots open."

"I don't suppose you'd be willing to combine it with Light Water Aerobics on Wednesdays?" Hunt asked.

"The dog could probably handle it, but it's definitely beyond your scope," Rufus replied in all seriousness.

CHAPTER TEN

"WHAT A COMMUNITY," Penny marveled after Rufus had made his goodbyes. "You meet such interesting people, all so involved."

"Education. The wellspring of life—for men and dogs," Ben said, not bothering to hide his amusement.

"Now that we've added that to your dance calendar, Hunt Phox, maybe you could make further amends and take out the trash. Matt can hold the dog," Katarina ordered.

"What is this? Beat up on Hunt night?" Hunt asked, feeling beleaguered. He gave Matt the leash, and miraculously, Fred seemed to have finally grown tired and lay down at his feet.

"Never mind, I'll take care of it. It's garbage pick-up tomorrow, so I need to put the cans down at the end of the driveway, anyway," Ben said. He smiled slyly at Hunt. "You stay and get beat up some more."

"Speaking of the dog, I think it's time to take him for a walk," Matt chimed in. Fred wagged his tail, twitching his behind, and practically dragged Matt out the back door.

"Trust a teenager to know when to get going," Hunt said. He looked at Julie and nodded at her wineglass. "Is there any more where that came from? I think I need some fortification."

"Here, you can have this glass. I poured it when I couldn't find my old one, and I haven't drunk from it yet."

Sarah rubbed her head. "I think I need to sit down again. If no one minds, I think I'll just curl up on the couch with Quiltie and have a little nap."

"Sit down, but hold off falling asleep. We have an important matter to discuss." Julie walked into the living room and sat on the coffee table facing Sarah. "You know what this is about, don't you?"

Sarah glanced at Hunt. "And *you* thought you needed fortification."

"Is something wrong, dear, something you haven't told me?" Penny asked anxiously.

Lena moved supportively next to Penny. "It's to do with her fainting, am I right?"

"It's nothing, Lena. I'm just tired tonight, a little over-heated," Sarah said.

Penny looked to Julie. "She's all right, isn't she? Just a little light-headed with the pregnancy? Even I fainted at your wedding."

"I think the circumstances were, uh, different," Julie said with more tact than she was usually known for. " I didn't want to put a damper on the earlier festivities, but now it's time to have a heart-to-heart. Just as a precaution, Sarah, I want you to come to the office so I can run some tests—sooner rather than later."

Sarah rolled her eyes. "But I'm booked solid in the coming weeks—clients at the office and a full slate of clients at the hospital."

"Tomorrow. Monday at the latest. No excuses. Even if there is nothing out of the ordinary, your fainting is not to be taken lightly."

"I know, I know. You explained back at the salon about pregnancy and blood pressure."

"Excuse me. I haven't finished."

Penny bit her lip. "Listen to Julie, Sarah. She *is* the doctor after all."

"Yes, Mother." Sarah never called her mother "Mother" unless she was irritated.

"And don't forget what she told you about lying down," Katarina added.

"I know, I know, first sit a few minutes and then stand. And before you repeat any more of Julie's instructions, I remember the part about making sure to sleep on my side—" she held up her hand when Katarina was about to clarify, yet again "—on my *left* side because in the third trimester my gi-normous uterus—"

"It's not that big, Sarah." Her mother tried to comfort her.

Sarah held her tongue but muscled to sit up straight. "Whoops!" The abrupt shift left her a little woozy, and she leaned against the arm of the couch.

"Oh dear, this is serious." Penny frowned and bit her lip.

Julie continued. "About eight percent of pregnant women develop a condition when they lie on their back called supine hypotensive syndrome—increased heart rate, drop in blood pressure. They may experience nausea, anxiety and light-headedness." She brought her head menacingly close to Sarah. "Sound familiar?"

"You can't scare me." Sarah lifted her chin.

Julie gave her the evil eye. Coming from a Sicilian family, she was an expert. "You should be. Okay, you can remedy the situation by taking precautions, but what happens if you have one of these spells, say, behind the wheel of a car?"

Sarah dismissed her question with the wave of her hand. "Really, the likelihood of something like that is so minimal."

"Are you sure? Would that be your explanation to the family of someone whose car you ran into after you lost control? Do you want to risk your life and the life of your unborn fetus, let alone gamble with someone else's life?" Julie's voice was chilling.

Sarah looked into her friend's eyes and was shocked to see how serious she was. She had known Julie for all the time she had lived in Grantham, roughly four years. In many ways she knew her intimately—what she thought of their various colleagues, her favorite ice cream, and her nervous habit of twiddling a lock of hair around her index finger when she was reading. But this was different, and even though she had no proof, she was sure that Julie's dire warnings rose out of something deeply personal.

"Okay, I grant you that there might be a remote possibility that I could faint when driving, but in all seriousness, what do you intend for me to do about it?" Sarah asked.

Julie put her hands together as in prayer. "Please, for a smart woman you can be so dense!" She spread her arms apart in exasperation. "How do I say this? I've never lost a patient in labor, but I've had two die driving to the hospital. I don't want the same thing happening to you before you even get that far. In two words, stop driving." She glowered at Sarah.

"Stop driving! I can't possibly give up driving,"

Sarah protested. "Almost a third of my patients are post-operative home visits."

"Then you'll have to give them up." Julie crossed her arms in front of her chest.

"But I can't just give them up! It's my job! For a smart woman, *you* can be so dense. Do I need to remind you that I need to support myself and my unborn child?"

"Then you'll just have to get someone to drive you," Katarina said, shaking her head.

"Hello, I can't afford a limousine service." Sarah's voice rose. "Not unless I want to give up little things like food and utilities."

"I suppose there's always Zach, dear," Penny said tentatively, referring to Sarah's ex-fiancé.

Sarah looked at her aghast.

Penny stood her ground. "Don't look at me that way. After all, he was intimately involved in making the baby, or so you said."

"Who's Zach?" Hunt asked Lena quietly.

"You mustn't mention the name Zach." Lena covered her mouth with her hand. Even so, her powerful voice penetrated across the room.

Sarah blew out her breath loudly. "Mother, if I said Zach was the biological father, then Zach was the biological father. I do not sleep around!"

Penny covered her mouth.

"Secondly—" Sarah was not done, no, sirree "—under no circumstances will I contact Zach, and that's final."

"I don't get it." Hunt took a thoughtful sip of wine, finishing off the glass. "If this guy is the father, why doesn't she call him?" he asked Katarina.

"It's complicated," Katarina explained under her breath. "I'll tell you later."

"Then you'll just have to find someone else to help out," Julie said, bringing the conversation back to the issue at hand. "I would gladly let you move in with me, but my hours aren't remotely compatible with yours, and I just don't have the flexibility to drive you when you need to see patients."

"And we live out in the boonies," Katarina said. "You couldn't even walk anywhere."

"You are more than welcome to stay with me," Lena offered. "At least my house is within walking distance of the hospital and your office. And I suppose I could always rearrange my volunteering schedule and classes, and…oh, yes…my tennis games until the baby comes."

"Don't be ridiculous," Sarah protested. "That would be much too much of an inconvenience." Besides, she had seen the way Lena drove. Talk about risking life and limb on a daily basis. She held up her hands to try to establish some order. "Listen, everybody, really, you're more than generous, but clearly none of you has the time or the lifestyle or…whatever to make it all work."

Penny cleared her throat.

"Yes, Mother?" Sarah snapped, losing her patience. She heard Lena breathe in sharply. Sarah sighed, realizing she had sounded mean. "Sorry, Mom, I'm just tired. You had something to say?"

"I was supposed to leave tomorrow. Your lovely friend Katarina is taking me to the airport. But under the circumstances, I think the best solution is for me to call your father and tell him I'm staying here with you until the baby comes," Penny said.

"Mom, that's really sweet of you to offer, but you're

afraid to drive on Route One, and you don't know how to parallel park. What would you do in town?"

"I could learn."

"But you know that Dad will starve if you're not there to shop and cook."

"That's not true. He's quite fond of Applebee's, even if it is a bit pricey for our budget." Penny paused. "I know, he could come out here with me for part of the time. I'm sure he wouldn't mind."

Sarah held up her hand. "Mom. Mom," she repeated. "I love you dearly, I really do. So I love you enough to tell you that while your offer is really and truly generous, we both know it would never work. First of all, I live in a one-bedroom apartment."

She held up her hand when Penny was about to object. "And, no, you and Dad cannot sleep on the floor, and I can barely get up off the floor at this point, so that's out. Besides, we both know that we can't live under the same roof for more than three days max. After that, I would be worried that Dad would be bored or anxious about the farm, or that you would think my baseboards weren't clean enough."

"I always did prefer a wet cloth over a dry one," Penny commented.

"What's a baseboard?" Hunt asked.

No one listened. Except Lena. She walked closer to him, stood on tiptoe and tapped him on the upper arm, the same arm that was now holding an empty glass.

Hunt looked down.

"Never mind the baseboards," she said. She looked at him through narrowed eyes, and then began lurching her head repeatedly to the side.

"I'm sorry. Do you need something?"

"Young people these days," Lena muttered, and kicked him in the shin.

"Ow!" Hunt said loudly.

Katarina snapped her fingers. "I've got it."

Lena breathed a sigh of relief. "Finally!"

Katarina climbed over Julie's long legs and sat on the coffee table in front of Sarah. "I don't know why I didn't think of it sooner. What about Hunt here? He'd be perfect. You already know each other, and as far as I can tell, he's not doing a thing."

"What do you mean I'm not doing anything? Just because I've given up wearing a watch and carrying a BlackBerry doesn't mean I'm not busy. Look, I—I have a new dog to take care of," Hunt stammered. He stared longingly at his empty wineglass.

Katarina looked over. "Oh, come off it, Hunt. It's as clear as daylight that you're drifting. I went through a long rehab, too, and I know what it feels like. But I can also appreciate how important it is to trust the instincts of those who care about you."

Ben walked in rubbing his hands together. "It's cold out there." He surveyed the faces in the room. "By the looks of things, it's not exactly cozy in here, either."

Katarina reached out and he came to stand next to her. She grabbed his fists and kissed them lightly. She looked at him and a silent communication passed between them. Then she turned back to Hunt and confronted him squarely in the eye. "Do it."

Hunt shifted his gaze to Ben. "You're just in time to protect me from your wife and her good intentions."

"My wife's a smart woman. I agree with whatever she says," Ben said without even knowing the details.

Katarina patted him on the arm. "Hunt, what do you say?"

"Huntington, my boy, you realize you have no choice in the matter, don't you?" Lena said.

Hunt threw up his hands.

IT'S ONLY A MATTER OF a few weeks, he told himself. *You won't see her most of the day. But what about the nights?*

Didn't anyone think that maybe he purposely chose to live by himself? That he didn't necessarily want to share the events of his day over dinner? *Dinner!* The idea of food roiled his tender stomach.

He narrowed his eyes at Katarina and Ben, shifted his surly gaze to Lena, and totally avoided the glower from Julie sitting opposite Sarah.

Sarah.

He didn't know what to think of Sarah. Maybe chatting with her wouldn't be so bad. Maybe she'd even make a cherry pie every once in a while. That, his stomach could handle. Okay, he could do this.

He fisted his hands. "Listen, I guess, if you're looking for a convenient place to hang your hat, my place should fit the bill. I live right in town, and the house is big enough for more than two people. And I can probably drive you during the day, if you need a lift someplace or other."

"Excuse me," Sarah interjected. "You don't need to do that," she said to Hunt. "And you all, maybe I'd like to have a say in the matter? And my say is, 'no.'"

Penny scanned Hunt up and down. "But, Sarah, how can you refuse? It seems like such a perfect solution, and

he seems to be a very nice person, even if he is a...a...
man."

"Just a minute. After being practically railroaded
into this whole thing, you're now saying you don't want
to live with me because I'm a man? Is that what your
mother meant?"

Sarah expelled a large breath upward, sending her
bangs flying. "What my mother was trying to imply, and
because you're bound to find out soon enough anyway,
given this crowd—"

Everyone besides Hunt acted as if they didn't know
what she was talking about.

She ignored them and addressed Hunt. "You see,
I don't especially have a great track record with men,
especially my ex-fiancé who only revealed on the day
of our wedding that he was gay."

"I'd say that's a bit of an understatement," Julie
said.

Sarah shot her a what-gives glance. "Thank you, my
dearest friend."

Hunt digested this news for a few moments. "Oh. So
you're not gay?"

Sarah shook her head. "No. But even if I were gay,
what difference would it make?"

"None." Well, there were obvious differences from
his perspective, but he was not going to elaborate. He
felt an unexpected relief and a sudden burst of happiness.
And confusion....

"Wait a minute. Why am I the one sounding defen-
sive? If it doesn't make any difference if you're gay or
straight, why does it matter what Zach's preferences are?
That was your fiancé's name, right?"

Sarah waved him over, and he settled on the arm of the couch next to her.

She lowered her voice. "It has nothing to do with the fact that he's gay. All right, it does, because I thought he was in love with me, and it turns out he wasn't…well… not in the way he pretended to be. Essentially, he lied. He lied to me." Sarah pressed her index finger to her heart.

"Sounds to me that he was lying to himself, living a lie," he whispered back.

Sarah wrestled with his words. "Okay, maybe. I don't know. But that still doesn't condone his sneaking around. Or the fact that he was doing it with another guy on the day of our wedding."

That admission had Hunt opening his mouth, speechless.

"I mean, what kind of cruel person does that?"

Hunt frowned and scratched the side of his neck. He opened his hand beseechingly. "Maybe someone who wanted to be caught? Because he knew he couldn't go on living a lie, but didn't have the courage or know how to tell you?"

Sarah threw up her hands. "Argh! You're so understanding! I can't stand it!" She didn't bother to keep her voice down. "Listen, I'm sure there's some truth in what you say, but that still doesn't excuse the fact that he hurt me. Hurt me by cheating on me, especially on a day that meant so much to my family."

"And to you, as well?" Hunt prompted.

"And to me, as well," Sarah repeated, but without the same vigor.

"So, why don't you take my help? Are you saying *I'm* the problem?" Hunt felt put out. He stood.

"I think it's more like she's the problem," Julie interrupted. "Sarah's more than willing to help the whole world, but try and lend her a hand? Listen, Sarah, this is me, your friend *and* your obstetrician talking. Take the offer." Julie nodded perfunctorily at Hunt. "If a better one appears on the horizon, fine, but for now, I don't think you have any choice."

Hunt crossed his arms.

"Hey," Julie began, "I'm sure you're a perfectly nice guy. Anyway, we all know your mother lives in town, and she would never let you behave like anything other than the perfect gentleman."

"How nice that you live near your mother," Penny said cheerfully.

"Why does that sound like a criticism of me?" Sarah said to no one in particular.

Julie patted her hand. "Get over it. We all feel that way about our mothers. We can't help it. When we have daughters, they'll feel the same way about us." She raised her head to Hunt. "You appear to have your own issues to deal with at the moment. You think you can handle the pressure?"

"Pressure. You want pressure. Not only am I somehow signed up for a water aerobics class, I've now got myself going to a dog training class. What's opening my house up to an almost complete stranger got to compare with those two things?"

"Hardly a complete stranger. After all, you've seen her in a bikini," Lena pointed out.

Hunt blinked, the image flashing before his eyes. "That's true." He paused, recalling each notable detail. Then he shook his head and focused on the here and now.

"Whatever. So tell me—on top of those responsibilities, are there any other obligations that someone has yet to tell me about?"

CHAPTER ELEVEN

SARAH GAZED AROUND the entrance of Hunt's ultra-modern home. "This isn't a house. It's more like the lobby of some boutique hotel. You know, Katarina mentioned that Ben's business partner had this amazing place, but I never expected this."

Hunt's house—*castle* was a more apt word, Sarah thought—was a postmodern gray-stone monolith. Three stories tall, it loomed on the edge of the university campus in stark contrast to the neighboring clapboard houses and the engineering school's sixties, blah brick building, which could easily have been mistaken for a box store.

The house had a massive double-door entryway with a broken pediment above. The ground floor windows were long narrow slits that looked perfect for pouring forth boiling oil on any passing horde.

Hunt, Sarah and Fred stood inside the entryway—"foyer" Hunt had called it. The dog strained on his leash, his nails scratching on the polished floors in a furious tattoo. A painting on the wall caught Sarah's eye. She shifted the KitchenAid mixer in her arms. "That's by someone famous, isn't it?" she said.

"Joan Miró."

"Right." Sarah nodded slowly. She was getting the feeling that she wasn't in rural Minnesota anymore.

"There was a show of his at the Museum of Modern Art. Katarina and I took the train in to see it."

"Yes, I saw it, too. I think this one is better than a lot of the pieces they had hanging." He cleared his throat. Fred yanked on his leash again. Hunt rested Sarah's duffel bag on the bottom rung of a suspended spiral staircase that seemed to float upward to some Busby Berkeley heaven. "Listen, I need to take him out for a short walk before I let him have the run of the house."

"Sure, you wouldn't want him lifting his leg on anything like that." With a shake of her head, she indicated a geode the size of a lunar landing module. "That could be a bitch to clean."

"You're right. My cleaning lady would probably up and quit, and that would be a disaster."

"I can imagine. How do you dust a geode, anyway?"

"Don't ask me. I don't even know how the washing machine runs." Hunt pointed over his shoulder. "I'll be less than a minute. Why don't you just put down that… that…" He waggled his hand toward the mixer in her arms.

"Mixer. It's a mixer," she explained.

"Right, whatever it is, it looks heavy. Just put it down for now. I still can't believe you insisted on bringing that but only a small duffel bag of clothes."

"Well, I needed the essentials. And can you bring in the box with the kitchen supplies when you come back?"

"No problem," he said over his shoulder. Fred had already pulled him out the front door. "Just take the elevator upstairs meanwhile. Fred always does. And put your feet up." The door closed behind him with a whisper and then a thud.

Sarah sank on a lower step of the cantilevered stairway and eased the mixer to the floor. She gazed down. "Marble," she noted. "Great for baking."

She lowered her chin to her cupped fingers and stared around the place. What was she doing in a house with priceless art and an elevator? She peered more closely at the stairs. "Nah, it can't possibly just lift up, can it?"

Then she noticed what looked like a futuristic light switch embedded in the bamboo paneling—so ecologically minded it practically screamed smugness. Though, Sarah had to admit, it did look pretty nice. Still, she wasn't game enough to press it and find out what would happen. With her luck she'd probably cause an alarm system to go off.

"But, you know," she said out loud, her voice echoing in the elegant, deserted environment, "hasn't my life already set off an alarm system?"

And then the walls started to shake.

"I THINK THIS ONE IS BETTER than the ones they have hanging in the show," Hunt mumbled to himself, repeating his earlier words. He watched Fred lift a leg on a privet hedge outside the engineering library. "Jeez, what a snooty thing to say."

Somehow after Sarah had maneuvered herself into the low bucket passenger seat in the Porsche, and they'd wrangled Fred into the tiny back cavity of the 911, the full impact of what he'd just agreed to do finally sank in. He had agreed, or rather been railroaded, into living 24/7 with a voluptuous woman who was soon to give birth to another man's baby.

Not exactly what he would have predicted five years ago, let alone yesterday or even this morning.

Ever since college, Hunt had lived alone. On purpose. Oh, he was social enough, never at a loss for an invitation, date or an affair. Popularity was something that came easily to him. Just like the rest of his life.

Maintaining a lasting relationship was another thing, and he didn't mean getting together with his old Grantham University roommates for reunions each year. That type of camaraderie came easily to him. All it required was a good memory for names, a relatively quick wit and freely flowing alcohol.

As far as he could tell, the only true friend he had was Ben. And while he trusted him without reserve, and the two had weathered good times and bad, he couldn't really say they were close. He was more than happy to listen to Ben bare his soul, but the probability of him sitting down for a heart-to-heart about his inner angst was just about nil. About as likely as him having children.

And he wasn't even referring to the possibility of shooting blanks after going through chemo. That was one of the upsides of his treatment, his oncologist had explained to him. No, as any self-respecting psychiatrist could have told him—not that he would ever see one—his reluctance to commit to anything resembling a long-term relationship with a woman stemmed back to his childhood. *Well, duh*, Hunt would have replied.

Others, and even he, laughed at his overbearing mother who gave singular meaning to the term *doyenne*. *Diva* didn't even come close. But he was no mamma's boy, not even close. Other people buckled under Iris's iron will and did what she "recommended." Hunt, by contrast, just listened to her thinly veiled orders, and then turned around and did just what he pleased.

Besides, the real source of his personal hang-ups wasn't his mother.

It was his father.

It was a secret Hunt kept to himself, not out of deference to the hallowed memory of his late father, but to preserve the life his mother had created for herself and, as a consequence, him. As Hunt knew only too well, Iris's insistence on total and absolute control was nothing more than a defense mechanism born out of a marriage that had left her powerless and unloved.

Hunt's solution was different. Besides the irrepressible urge to banter, Hunt made sure to distance himself from intimacy. On second thought, the banter accomplished that, as well.

So was it any surprise now that intimacy had been forced upon him—even without an emotional, romantic component—he found himself pushing back? Hunt looked down and realized that Fred had finally stopped anointing the bushes and was busy chewing on the plastic covering of a bicycle lock. It might be a losing endeavor, but he seemed to be enjoying the process.

Maybe that was the tack he should take with his new roommate. Quit trying to fight it and just enjoy whatever small benefits that came from being a good Samaritan.

Anyway, it wasn't as if they were required to form a close personal bond. He would merely be her driver. She could just text him when she needed a lift, and he could come and get her. If he had to wait around at all, he could read the paper, or better yet, use the time to decide how he was going to "improve society." Along those lines, he was beginning to view these chauffeur duties as a kind of community activism, a volunteer job. As the saying went, charity begins at home, and what better charitable project than opening up his own home?

In the meantime, seeing as she said she wasn't interested in getting into a personal relationship, he could start practicing his social skills again, with no risk of commitment.

Hunt smiled. He liked that idea. Liked it very much. He could practice all his usual wiles, knowing that nothing would ever come of it, but at the same time reaping long-term benefits—a sound investment strategy if ever there was one. Then at the end of these few remaining weeks, he would wish her well with her new baby, even give her a generous and thoughtful gift. He could even imagine visiting the two of them every once in a while, maybe playing with the baby. Not that Hunt had the faintest idea what one did with a newborn baby, but he was sure with online research he'd be just as equipped as the next person. After all, once upon a time, everything had always proved easy to him. And it was time to recapture that same feeling.

"Come, Fred. Let's move the car off the street and park it in the garage," Hunt said, feeling a renewed spring to his step. He even whistled a few off-key bars of Brahms's *Academic Festival Overture*.

Hunt beeped his Porsche unlocked and Fred hopped in front. He started the ignition and hung an illegal right turn into the one-way alley that provided access to the garage. He activated the remote and an industrial-strength, high-tech steel door rumbled open.

Hunt edged the car into the narrow space, then looked

across at the dog. "Come, Fred. Maybe if you're lucky she'll let you lick a beater when she uses that mixer to make a cake."

CHAPTER TWELVE

HUNT INCHED OPEN THE DOORWAY from the garage to the hallway. Juggling two boxes of kitchen supplies, one atop the other, he craned his neck to the side to see where he was going as he made his way to the foyer.

What he saw was Sarah brandishing the beater. He dropped Fred's leash and the dog scampered ahead, circled Sarah gleefully and gave a "hello" bark before racing up the stairs. His paws maybe hit every third step.

Sarah stood there, her arm aloft like the Statue of Liberty. She moved her eyes from Hunt to Fred and back to Hunt. Awkwardly, she lowered her arm. "I didn't know what was going on. Who was trying to get in by—by— What I mean to say is I heard this massive rumbling noise, and I thought maybe—maybe…"

"There'd been an alien invasion?" Hunt asked. "As much as I like the idea of you defending the house by whipping up a quick soufflé, I'm afraid it was just the sound of my industrial-strength garage door." He tried pressing the switch by leaning into it with his shoulder, but it was difficult to maneuver with precision. "Could you push the elevator button for me?"

"Oh, sure." She placed the beater on the top box and took it from him. "I wasn't sure exactly what to do, so I thought I'd just wait. I guess Fred is much more accustomed to the place."

"Actually, this is the first time he's used the stairs. He must have figured out what they were all about at Ben's."

The paneling drew back when Sarah pressed the button, and Hunt had her go in first. "I'll get the other stuff after I've shown you to your room. Meanwhile, just press two."

"Two?"

"Yeah, there's a bedroom and bathroom on this floor, along with the garage and storage and laundry rooms. But one floor up is the living room and dining room and kitchen. We can dump this stuff there."

Quickly, the small, paneled elevator whisked them up a floor. The doors opened, and Sarah stepped out. "Wow," she said, looking around, her mouth open.

The open space was a light-filled showroom of white-marble floor tiles, low Danish modern furniture, and industrial lighting. She did a three-sixty, taking in the wall of windows over the shaded side street, before focusing on the rest of the decor. There was a sleek, glass dining table and molded chairs, and a glossy white galley kitchen separated from the rest of the space by a white marble island. The stainless steel appliances were all high-end. And except for the front section of today's *New York Times,* there wasn't a thing—not a bowl of fruit, not a dirty coffee mug, not a box of Cheerios— sitting on the acre of white countertop.

Sarah winced. "I'm not sure my stuff is going to fit in with the decor."

"I'll just have to call my decorator and have her come over and instruct us where to put everything."

She looked at him askance. "You're joking, right?"

"I lay awake at night worrying about storage," Hunt teased. He stepped around her and rested the box on the counter. "Here, let me take that." He removed the one from her arms. "You can keep your stuff out on the counter if it's easier. It will add to the postindustrial charm of the place."

Sarah walked over and studied a large abstract oil painting hung above a low bookcase. It was a jumble of drips and blobs. "KitchenAid and Jackson Pollock. I never envisioned the two of them together." She turned back. "That is by Pollock, isn't it?" She pointed over her shoulder with her thumb.

"If I told you I bought it at the same time as a wastepaper basket from Target, would it seem less extravagant?"

"No, but I'd believe it." Then she noticed the twisted glass lighting fixture over the dining room table. Its undulating tubes of bright reds and oranges looked like a swirling sea creature from a coral reef. She pointed upward. "And that's by that famous glass guy, Dale Something, right?"

"Dale Chihuly, yes. You know a lot about art then?"

"Some. I lived in New York for a while, and going to museums and art galleries on weekends became my guilty pleasure. Well, not that guilty—I stuck to waste-paper baskets from Target."

Hunt laughed. "We'll have to compare. I'm sure it's charming. Anyway, one good thing about the Chihuly piece—it's up out of Fred's reach. Speaking of Fred, where has the monster gone?" Hunt asked. He glanced around, but didn't have to look far.

"Fred!" he thundered.

The dog was sitting smack-dab in the middle of a low black leather couch, his tail wagging, slapping quietly each time it made contact with the buttery-soft hide. Sarah could just imagine how his nails would go right through with very little effort.

"Fred!" Hunt shouted again. "You know that's out of bounds. Off!" He gave the dog a furious look, and the mutt reluctantly hopped off, only to rush across the floor, up the stairway by the kitchen, then a few seconds later, run down again. He sat up proudly in front of Hunt.

With what looked like a very expensive men's loafer in his mouth.

Hunt winced. "I would say it's wonderful that he's conquered his fear of stairs, but now it only opens up new opportunities to do evil. I have a solution, though. Food! What this dog needs is his dinner."

"What this dog needs is obedience classes."

"I know, I know. But first things, first. There's a bathroom down the back—" he pointed over his shoulder "—but the bedrooms are up another flight. As Fred has demonstrated, there're the stairs. Otherwise we can take the elevator."

"The stairs are fine. Listen, just give me directions, and I can find it myself. That way you can take care of the dog before he destroys something else."

"Okay, if you don't mind. My bedroom is to the left, facing the side street, but there're two bedrooms down the hall to the right. One's a study, but the other should work for you. It's got a connecting bathroom with towels and toiletries if you want to freshen up."

Sarah held the brushed steel handrail and trudged up the stairs. She nearly stumbled when she realized the drawings marching up the wall were the original artwork from *New Yorker* cartoons. She remembered decorating the makeshift bathroom in the illegal loft in Queens with ripped covers from the same magazine.

She reached the top of the stairs. She knew he said to turn right, but she couldn't resist sneaking a peek into the master bedroom. Besides, the door was open. *Maybe I just confused my right with my left,* she said, not really needing to justify her nosiness. She stopped. *Wow!*

The master bedroom ran the width of the house and had a wall of glass along the side street and a large platform bed—endlessly large. Only good manners, and the knowledge that Hunt might come up at any minute, kept her from investigating if the sheets were black.

She turned the other way along the hall and spied a smaller room to the right. Streetlamps shone through two long windows and illuminated the outlines of the sparse furnishings. She switched on the lights. Recessed lighting bathed the queen-size bed covered with a puffy, white duvet and a mountain of pillows. There were built-in closets, a low white dresser and a comfy uphol-stered armchair with a woven throw over one arm. A tall glass vase filled with branches of bittersweet sat on one end of the dresser.

Sarah slipped her small sports knapsack off her shoul-der onto the dresser. The room was perfectly lovely, if a little soulless, much like the rest of the house. But it was home for her for the next month or so. It could be worse, a lot worse.

She wandered to the adjoining bathroom that had a glass shower stall with glass-tiled walls. The marble sink was atop a Shaker-style vanity, compact but elegant.

She turned on the faucet and bent her head, cupping the water in her hands to splash her face. She reached for one of the incredibly plush white towels hanging from a heated towel rack and patted her face. Then she faced the mirror of the medicine chest.

She looked like crap. No, not that bad, just exhausted after a long day and evening. At least the twin lights over the mirror were forgiving enough not to highlight her pregnancy pimples.

She left the towel on the sink, not having the energy to hang it back up, and shuffled back to the bedroom. She pried off her shoes without bothering to undo the laces and stared at the bed. It wasn't a difficult choice to lie down.

Sarah adjusted the pillows behind her head and rested one on her belly. *I must remember to get out Quiltie,* she told herself. She yearned for something that was hers.

"What have I gotten myself into?" she asked out loud. She hugged the pillow and stared at the ceiling, the white paint a flawless abyss of minimalist chic, and replayed the evening's events.

Clearly, from his initial comments, Hunt was chafing under the bit. Just as clear was that they were as different as chalk and cheese. This house said it all. And to give him some excuse, she *had* been foisted on him without much choice on his part.

She also knew that for better or worse, they both had to make the best of the situation. She might not be any happier than he was, but Sarah was determined to act civilly until the baby came or preferably, until she came up with another idea. After all, it's not as if by temporarily moving in, she was making any kind of emotional commitment. At best you could describe their arrangement as roommates of convenience. *That's what we are,* Sarah decided. *Roommates.*

Besides, not to be totally self-centered, he was going through a difficult time, too. She might be about to have a baby all on her own, but he was grappling with life-and-death issues—all on *his* own. Maybe it wouldn't hurt her to reach out to him then, provide some respite from her own self-doubts and fears?

With more effort than she wanted to admit, Sarah swung her legs to the side of the bed and, grabbing on to the side table, swiveled to an upright position. The room swam a little—not so bad this time—and she followed Julie's instructions to take her time before standing up.

By the time she padded down the stairs in her bare feet she saw that Hunt had unpacked her boxes, but the contents lay strewn on the island.

He looked up as she approached. "I wasn't quite sure where to put things. My experience in the kitchen is pretty much limited to pressing the power button on the microwave, using the wine cooler and opening the refrigerator door. Oh, yes, and the freezer for ice." He picked up her tomelike copy of the Escoffier Cookbook and asked, "What is this? The baker's bible?"

"Don't even joke about something so sacred." She swiped the book from his hand and rested it safely on the countertop. "Some people jog to relax or do crossword puzzles or watch kung fu movies. I bake."

"Didn't you ever hear of drinking? Speaking of which, would you care for some wine?" He turned around and opened the wine cooler beneath the counter.

"No, thanks. Alcohol is a no-no during pregnancy."

Hunt frowned. "Of course. Sorry about that."

"But you can have a glass."

"No, that's all right. How about something along the lines of…" He examined various small containers that he'd unloaded from her boxes. "Here's something called 'Sleepy Time' tea. The bears in the picture on the box look very content, so it must be good."

Sarah laughed. "Yes, it's my nighttime ritual."

"Then by all means. I'll just put some water in the kettle. That much I can do. You can get the mugs down from the overhead cabinet by the dishwasher.

"Listen," he continued as he busied himself filling the Michael Graves kettle from the sink tap and igniting a gas burner on the stove, "I want to apologize for my behavior when we first got here. I think I started freaking out a bit. It's one thing to tell everyone that you're happy to help out, but it's another, once you get home… to realize—"

"That you're actually saddled with a complete stranger?" Sarah lined the mugs up side by side and opened the box of tea bags.

Hunt turned around, took off his glasses and rested them on the counter. "I wouldn't put it exactly like that."

"But then again…" Sarah glanced around, sensing something was missing. *That's right.* "Where's Fred?"

"He finally succumbed to exhaustion and is asleep on his bed in the corner by the couch." The teakettle whistled. Hunt poured the water into the cups. Silently, they watched the tea brew.

"Sugar?" Hunt asked nervously. "I'm sorry, I don't have any milk." He pulled out a slim drawer for spoons.

"No, thanks. I just take it plain. Do you have a small bowl or something I can save this in?" She held up her tea bag on her spoon.

"Here, I'll throw it into the garbage under the sink."

"Actually, I like to reuse my tea bags since I don't like my tea too strong."

Hunt looked at her with wide eyes. "I'm sure that's very admirable, a very 'waste not, want not' philosophy and all. But I think as long as you're staying here, we can afford to go a bit wild and only use them once." Hunt whisked away her tea bag and threw his away, too. Then he raised his hand toward the living room. "Shall we?"

"Okay." Sarah took her mug and followed him over. She studied the low, straight couch and the armchair that slanted back.

"I think the couch might be the best bet for you. I can probably find some pillows if you want."

"That's okay. I've got a few pillows at my apartment that Julie needlepointed for me. Maybe I can bring them over?" She eased herself down on the corner of the couch, and took a sip of her tea.

"Julie and needlepoint? Why does that seem like such an oxymoron?" He sat in the bowed-steel armed chair with a casual grace, and flopped one leg over the other, resting his ankle atop the opposite knee. "Speaking of your apartment, what about getting some more of your stuff, as well. I don't know, perhaps you need another pair of shoes, more flour? That lovely bathing suit of yours?"

Sarah moaned. "Please, don't remind me about the class." She took another sip of tea and thought about the logistics of her situation. "Let's see. Tomorrow's Friday, so I only need one day of work clothes, not that much fits me these days. Over the weekend, I'll probably call Katarina to have her pick me up to get some more of my stuff."

"Why call her? I can do it."

"Well, I'm sure you probably have better things to do over the weekend."

"I'm free, I promise."

"Well, for a second reason, your sports car is very nice, but I don't think the trunk and that itsy-bitsy backseat would fit much of my stuff. So, I thought Ben's Cherokee would be better."

"What about your car? You have a car, right?"

"Yeah, a four-year-old Honda Accord."

"Perfect! I can drive over to your place, load up your car and bring the stuff back here. Then, while you're unpacking, I'll drive it back and get my car. Simple, right?" Hunt drank some tea, then studied the remains in the mug. "Hey, this isn't bad. I could get to like it."

He sat forward and rested his mug on the glass coffee table between the couch and the chair. Sarah wanted to say something about coasters, but caught herself. His cleaning lady was probably a whiz with Windex.

Hunt got up and wandered to the low wooden bookshelves. He pushed aside some magazines and books and finally found what he wanted. His BlackBerry. "Why don't you give me your cell phone number?"

"I thought you'd given up wearing a watch and carrying a phone."

"I'll compromise. I'll leave the watch off but take the phone." He sat forward.

She rattled off her number.

He stared at his screen. "Wait a minute. I need my glasses. Now where did I put them?"

"I think you left them on the kitchen counter. You don't wear them all the time?"

He got up and retrieved them and settled them on his nose. "No, I only need them to read, but I tend to just keep them on because I keep forgetting where I put them down." He started tapping in her number.

"You don't need me to repeat it?" she asked.

"No, I've got it."

Sarah figured he probably *got* a lot of things if he was Ben's business partner.

"Done. When you go upstairs later, I'll call your phone, and then you'll have my number. That way you can call me when you need a ride."

Sarah finished her tea, but couldn't bring herself to put the cup on the beautiful coffee table. "You know, I think tomorrow I'll just walk into work. It's not that far from your house, and it'll be good exercise."

"Do you really think that's a good idea? I mean, as long as you're staying here I feel more or less responsible."

"I think 'less' is the operative word. Feel less responsible," Sarah said.

"Ha, easy for you to say. You're not the one who'll feel the full force of her wrath if anything goes wrong."

"Who? Your mother?"

"My mother? No, she's a pussycat by comparison. I'm talking about your doctor—the scary needlepointer."

Sarah crossed her arms, amused. "I think if push came to shove, you could probably go toe to toe with her. This bumbling rich kid act you put on isn't fooling me."

"It isn't? Too bad. I'm not used to being so transparent." He winked at her.

Sarah knew he was teasing, but a knot deep in her stomach tightened. She put her hand to her belly. The baby was high-fiving, too. She dropped her chin. *Don't jump to conclusions,* she quickly reminded herself. The guy was simply a natural born charmer. After all, she was pregnant for God's sake! Not exactly the greatest come-on.

"Actually, speaking of my mother, I suppose I should let her know sometime that you're staying here," Hunt said.

"From what I gather about your mother, you think she doesn't know already?"

Hunt nodded. "You're right."

They smiled at each other. Hunt drummed the tips of his fingers on the metal chair arm. Sarah stared out the window. The night was cloudless, the single streetlamp a soft glow illuminating the treetops from the other side of the street. If there'd been a clock in the room it would have been ticking. Loudly.

She glanced at Fred, curled up like a ball on his saggy cushion. "He's...ah...really asleep."

Hunt craned his neck to get a peek. "Yup, dogs'll do that."

"Listen," she said.

"You know," he said at the same time.

They cleared their voices.

"You first," Hunt offered.

Sarah bobbed her chin. "Okay. I just wanted to say that you don't have to feel obliged to entertain me or even spend much time with me. Just helping me get around is more than enough. I'm sure you have your own life, just like I have mine." Which at the moment, it was true, consisted of work, obstetrician appointments and trying to sleep.

"Naturally, I don't want to cramp your style," he said.

She snickered.

"But, really, I don't mind doing things together," Hunt added. "Maybe it sounds stupid, but maybe our time together could be a kind of social rehab after hibernating from chemo."

So she wasn't completely off the mark. Sarah felt relieved. She shook her head with a sense of purpose. Helping people was something she was good at. "In that case, the least I can do is show you how to get in shape and regain your strength. Maybe put on some muscle? You can think of me as a personal trainer, okay?"

They eyed each other, and Sarah was aware that what she was feeling was not the usual professional/client rapport. And the thought of what she *was* actually feeling? That had her more than a little afraid.

After a prolonged moment, Hunt broke eye contact. "I think this calls for a toast, don't you?" He reached over and raised his mug. "To new beginnings."

I can do this, she coached herself. Then she raised her mug. "To new beginnings."

Fred snored sublimely.

Hunt grinned. "And to a good Sleepy Time."

Sarah didn't want to think about her dreams.

CHAPTER THIRTEEN

"YOU MISSED A NICE get-together, Wanda," Rosemary, Sarah's office manager, said. She filled the drip coffeemaker with water from the carafe and then flicked the machine on. Wanda and Lena were the first appointments of the day, and they always came in early.

"Why I bother going to League of Women Voters' meetings when I know how New Jersey politics works is beyond me. Still, it's not like I didn't already hear all about the party." Wanda nodded to Lena sitting next to her in the waiting room. "I've got my own Katie Couric here, just as perky."

Lena, dressed in a navy blue warm-up outfit, was thumbing through a copy of *People*. "I must be really getting old. I don't recognize half the names of the people they're writing about." She flipped the magazine shut and looked up. "Please, you were the one who called me wanting to get the so-called 'inside scoop.' And those are her words and not mine, Rosemary," Lena added with a definitive nod. "What kind of coffee is that, anyway? It smells wonderful."

"Just the usual from Sam's Club." Rosemary pushed back the cuff of her violet-colored turtleneck sweater. The color complemented her nails with their air-brushed pansies and rhinestone accents. She glanced at her watch. "She's late, which isn't like her."

Rosemary's frown indicated concern. "I thought you said that Dr. Antonelli told her she couldn't drive anymore. You don't think something's happened?"

Wanda waved her hand in a calming motion. "Rosemary, remember your blood pressure. Take several deep, cleansing breaths." She turned toward Lena. "I thought you said you fixed everything with Iris's son, Huntington? You did, didn't you?"

Lena sighed. "The two of you, such mother hens. Forget those big breaths, Rosemary." She caught the receptionist mid-gulp. "I've got something much better." She reached for her purse, a Coach bag that Katarina had given her last Christmas. It was lovely, but much too expensive in Lena's opinion. "Here." She held out several Lindt truffles. "I've got dark chocolate. They're supposed to be very good for the heart."

"I shouldn't," Rosemary protested but quickly caved. She unwrapped the round candy and popped it in her mouth. "I feel better already," she said between swallows.

"Excuse me." Wanda wiggled her finger as Lena was about to put the chocolate away.

"Excuse *me,*" Lena said with mock horror. She set a chocolate in Wanda's outstretched hand. "And as to your worrying, don't. After the shower I got a text from Katarina that she saw her leave with him in that tiny sports car of his, with that crazy dog."

The mention of the word *dog,* made Wanda's shoulder bag, lying on the floor by her chair, start shaking.

Lena lifted her eyebrows. Why wasn't she surprised? Contrary to all regulations, numerous health codes and everyone's distress, Wanda insisted on carrying her lapdog, Tiger, with her wherever she went.

"As to Sarah's arrival, they should be here—" Lena checked at her very sensible Timex wristwatch "—in approximately three minutes." She tapped the crystal. "You know I got a new battery last week from the watch repairman at the Trenton Farmers' Market. What a bargain, and a genius of a man, in my opinion."

Wanda harrumphed. "We all know about your bargains. And pray, tell us how you are able to so accurately predict Sarah's ETA? Your new crystal is also a crystal ball?"

"There's a watch repairman at the farmers' market? I didn't know that," Rosemary said. She neatly folded her candy wrapper and looked at it longingly.

"Here, have one more," Lena offered, and dug in her bag. "And why I know what's going on is that while I was driving here earlier this morning, I saw them walking together."

"And they were coming in this direction?" Rosemary leaned over the counter that separated her desk from the carpeted reception area. Grantham Physical Therapy was a ground-floor space in a small office complex opposite the Grantham Shopping Center.

"Sarah was definitely walking in this direction, but that crazy dog of Huntington was pulling down some driveway. Which may explain why Sarah is late."

"Well, I think it's wonderful that she has company. What's a few minutes one way or the other?" Rosemary said.

"Tell that to the reservation desk at the tennis club," Wanda shot back.

"Ach, Wanda, I'm disappointed in you. Sometimes punctuality is not the first concern for a woman. Did you ever think that maybe Sarah likes being late on account of a man?"

"Oh, please, Lena. You of all people know a woman's first priority need not be a man. What did we fight for all those years ago?" Wanda didn't bother to wait for a reply. "We marched the streets so that a woman can do it all."

There was a decisive yip from her bag on the floor.

Wanda bent over and made a kissy-face with her lips. "That's my sweetness. What a good little doggy." She straightened up and looked from one woman to the other. "What? I can't be an ardent feminist and a dog lover?"

"Of course you can," Lena agreed. Though how anyone could love Tiger was beyond Lena. "And by the same token, Sarah can remain strong and independent but still be open to kindness and affection—and not just from dogs. After all, when we decided to sign her up for water aerobics, we had more than physical fitness in mind."

Rosemary nodded. "I couldn't agree more. She deserves the best, especially after that whole Zach thing."

All three women nodded their heads in agreement.

"So let's all try to be somewhat sympathetic when she comes in," Lena advised, especially to her friend. "Besides, Huntington is a nice boy. Very polite. Very smart. Sarah could do worse, far worse." She held up her hands. "But remember. Don't make a fuss over her. Everyone act very natural when she arrives."

There was the sound of footsteps scraping on the mat outside the door. All three watched as the door handle moved downward.

A BUZZER SOUNDED WHEN the door opened.

"Hi, everyone," Sarah said in greeting. Her cheeks had a rosy glow from the cool air. Fall had come early this mid-September morning.

"Hello," the three women chimed as one. Wanda stood ramrod straight, her hands clenched in fists by her sides. Lena made a show of flipping through a magazine. Rosemary rearranged the Sweet'n Low packets in the bowl by the coffee pot.

Sarah frowned. "Is something wrong? I know I'm a few minutes late. Sorry about that. We can run over the hour to make up for it."

"Late? You're late?" Lena looked at her wristwatch. "So you are! We didn't even notice, we were so busy chatting, weren't we?"

Rosemary nodded. "Chatting and talking..." Her voice trailed off.

Sarah angled her head to catch the title of Lena's magazine. *"Field and Stream?"*

"I'm thinking of taking a trip to Montana." Lena slapped the magazine shut. "I've never been out west to see the national parks, all the mountains."

"Who doesn't like the mountains?" Wanda said.

"So refreshing," Rosemary agreed.

Sarah looked at them all dubiously.

The buzzer went off again and Fred dashed into the reception area, pulling Hunt in his wake. He made a beeline for Wanda's satchel.

"Fred, Fred, stop," Hunt ordered between gasps. If Sarah had a healthy glow of fresh air and exercise, Hunt appeared as if he had just crossed the Sahara on an empty canteen. Sweat dripped from his forehead, and lines of strain marked his cheeks and the corners of his eyes.

"Huntington, how nice to see you," Lena said. "What a surprise!"

"Yes, what a surprise!" Wanda smiled brightly.

Now Sarah was *really* dubious.

Hunt waved. "Nice to see you, again, Mrs. Zemanova." He yanked Fred away from Wanda's canvas carryall. "Fred seems obsessed with what's in this bag. Bologna sandwich maybe? Beluga caviar?" He exhaled through his mouth, still out of breath.

Sarah eyed Wanda's bag with a raised eyebrow. "More like a sausage dog."

"With serious heartburn," Lena quipped.

"More like a serious time bomb waiting to go off," Rosemary suggested.

"Don't listen to them," Wanda cooed to her bag.

Everyone laughed but Hunt.

"Is there something I should be worried about?" Hunt asked.

Fred strained against his collar as Hunt held him away from the satchel. His front paws lifted off the ground, and he tried to dance forward on his back ones.

"Oh, I'd definitely be worried if I were you," Sarah said. She took a large step away from Wanda's bag.

And that's when it emitted a full-scale stink bomb.

CHAPTER FOURTEEN

WANDA'S BAG FLIPPED OVER and made snuffling noises.

Hunt twisted around to face at Sarah. "It's alive? I thought someone might have forgotten a doggie bag of shrimp cocktail—from last week."

"More like the doggy. Wanda, I don't like the sound of Tiger's breathing." Sarah walked toward the hall to her office. "And if you're going to have a meeting of canine minds, maybe you could do it outside?" she asked. It was a perfectly reasonable request, she told herself. And it also showed just how tired she was.

Last night she'd slept badly, and it wasn't just because pregnancy played havoc with her REM cycles. It was him. Hunt. Plain and simple. Only there wasn't anything plain or simple about him.

It was the hormones making her horny, she told herself. Under normal circumstances she'd never look twice at a rich-boy type—even if he did have those thoughtful frown lines and wore wire-rim glasses, with those intelligent gray-blue eyes. Never mind his charm. He could make her laugh when all she wanted to do was cry.

True, he wasn't exactly a specimen of manly health and vigor, but as she lay alone in bed, she could easily imagine him with a few more pounds—okay, more than a few. And if he started working out regularly the muscle mass would come back quickly on his long, lean frame, accentuating his natural grace.

Oh, my. How amazingly easy it was to conjure up the image.

How stupid, she told herself. Still, could she have been wrong about the sexual awareness that had passed between them last night when they were drinking tea?

Sarah had enough going on in her life without going there, she told herself. Hormones. No one could trust their instincts when their hormones were as out of whack as hers were.

Which was all perfectly logical, but tell that to her disjointed sleep patterns.

Under the circumstances, Sarah had done the only thing she could, short of barging into his bedroom, ripping off her Bart Simpson T-shirt and flannel pajama bottoms, launching herself onto his bed like the *Queen Mary* coming into dock, and exclaiming, "Take me."

Even Sarah wasn't that much of a fool.

Instead she baked. At two-thirty in the morning.

When he'd emerged from his bedroom and padded down the stairs wearing a pair of old gray sweatpants slung low on his hips, and a waffle-cotton Henley shirt with faded black lettering reading Grantham 150-Crew, she'd gulped her lukewarm herbal tea and knew she was a goner. God, she was beginning to hate herbal tea. What she wouldn't give for a double-shot espresso.

"Have a corn muffin. I baked them last night," she said, pushing her other thoughts to the very back of her mind.

He ran his hand through his hair, which was already standing up and should have looked a mess, but instead looked thicker and richer than just a few days ago, and yawned. "What a perfect way to start the day," he said with a crinkly smile. He breathed in deeply. "The smell of freshly baked breakfast, the sight of a beautiful woman."

That had Sarah snorting because she knew it was just rich-boy bull.

"And the promise of unadulterated caffeine." He headed as if guided by a homing device directly for the automatic espresso machine perched on the end of the counter and turned it on. The mechanical innards cranked to life. He grabbed a mug, placed it under the nozzles, and pressed the button. The smell of freshly brewed coffee permeated the room.

Hunt lifted the mug to his lips and closed his eyes while he took a sip. "Ah-h. Is there anything more wonderful than coffee in the morning?"

"I wouldn't know for more weeks than I care to count," she snapped back. Then she looked around, aware that something was missing. "Where's your side-kick? The furry one?"

"I hope Ben is still in bed with his lovely wife, Katarina."

She rolled her eyes. "Please, you know who I mean. The Demon of Fleet Street?"

"I believe the demon is still on my bed, chewing one of my old tennis shoes as we speak."

"Is that some indirect way of trying to get out of walking with me?"

"Not at all. It's a very direct way of allowing me to eat a muffin in peace. You can't get rid of me that easily."

He proceeded to drink coffee and inhale a muffin. He seriously eyed another before patting his concave waistline. "I better not. You know, next time you bake something, let me clean up afterward. It's the least I can do."

She'd nodded, and hated him all the more.

And now as she walked down the gray, carpeted hallway she was in no better mood. She'd been hoping that by setting a brisk pace he'd quickly beg off. But despite the fact that the dog had made a zigzag course, sniffing every blade of grass and leaf along the way, Hunt had kept up, occasionally making a witty comment or deriding his own pathetic lack of fitness.

If he'd been a client, she would have considered him a model patient, realistic about his status but determined to improve.

Only he wasn't a client. In fact, Sarah was having a hard time pigeonholing him as to what exactly he was.

Temporary necessity, she told herself, scowling as she bent over and pushed her sports knapsack into the bottom drawer of her desk. She slipped off her fleece vest, placed it neatly over the back of her swivel chair, and sat down.

From down the hall she could hear laughter and the light prancing of paws on the carpet. Evidently, Hunt and Fred were charming the ladies. She barely knew the guy and now he was insinuating himself into her work life. Next he'd be doing her laundry. No, his cleaning lady would be doing her laundry. While that didn't sound all that bad, she wasn't sure it was all that good, either. What had happened to her single-mom-to-be resolve that she could and would do it all herself?

Sarah rested a hand on her belly and focused on feeling her baby move. She closed her eyes and breathed in deeply. She was freaking out over really what was not a big deal, she reminded herself. *Relax*. The important thing was that she was doing the right thing in terms of having a healthy baby. So what if she was cranky, couldn't sleep, and dependent on someone else—let alone horny as all get-out.

She hypnotically rubbed circles over her rounded belly. She needed to cut herself some slack. Not think of everything as a battle, as a test of her strength and her determination to finally get something right—all on her own.

She heard a bark. And reluctantly got up, knowing she couldn't put off the start of her day even though she could have easily fallen asleep on one of the padded tables in the room. She didn't even need a table. Her chair would do just fine.

"In your dreams, Sarah Halverson," she said out loud and reached up to refix her ponytail. "You can do this," she told herself, marching down the hallway.

She turned the corner and saw Hunt leaning over the counter, cell phone in hand, talking to Rosemary. Lena was sitting in a chair with Fred partially hidden by one of her legs. He peaked out from behind her warm-ups as Tiger growled aggressively. Wanda purred. Lena patted Fred reassuringly.

"What a good puppy," Lena cooed at Fred, who began gnawing on her sneaker shoelace. She gently nudged him away. "You just need love and affection. Who knows what awful things someone did to you? Huntington, I am so proud of you for rescuing this poor creature."

Hunt grinned at Lena. "No biggie. And, Rosemary, thanks for the numbers." He offered her an equally dashing smile. Both women looked as if a temporary paralysis had gripped their euphoric expressions.

Wanda gave Tiger little kisses on his pointy nose, then addressed Hunt. "We'll have to set up dog playdates. I think it would definitely help with Fred's socialization. He clearly has so much potential."

Sarah groaned inwardly. They were *all* smitten. And here she thought of them as independent, strong-willed women. Give them a good-looking man with effortless charm and a puppy and they melted like Milky Way bars in the summer's heat.

"Ahem." She cleared her throat.

All three heads turned toward her, reluctantly.

"Oh, Sarah, Hunt and I have exchanged phone numbers in case of an emergency. Isn't that a good idea of his?" Rosemary fluttered her hands. The rhinestones on her nails sparkled under the fluorescent lights.

"Wonderful," Sarah said without much enthusiasm. She turned to Wanda and Lena. "So, if you two can tear yourselves away from the canine activities, we'll begin your sessions." She forced a smile.

Then she glanced at Hunt. He was leaning on an elbow against the counter. Over his shirt he had thrown on a North Face jacket, a combination of olive-green and gray that should have looked bilious but somehow was masculine and outdoorsy and even smelled of pine needles. She shook her head. Life was so unfair.

"Now that you have the office numbers, you can either call them or my cell to check on when I'll be done. That way you can walk over to meet me," she said. She could be unfair, too.

"I've got another idea. How about you call me when you're finished, and I'll drive to pick you up." Hunt pushed away from the counter.

She noticed he wasn't panting anymore and that his

skin no longer had a sheen of sweat. It did have a hint of dark-blond bristles, however, which only accentuated the craggy laugh lines in his cheeks. She cleared her throat.

"Don't tell me you're getting a cold?" Rosemary asked with concern.

Sarah patted her neck. "No, just a frog in my throat." Sarah turned back to Hunt again. "But I thought we'd agreed to walk both ways?"

"Sarah, don't you think since it's his first day it might be better to ease him into exercising gradually?" Rosemary said.

"Thank you, Rosemary, but I promised Hunt that as part of the bargain of staying at his place I'd get him in shape after his therapy."

She studied Hunt and was dismayed to find he was smiling at her. Oh, my God, she would quickly join the rest of them in their stupefaction if she weren't careful. "Besides, if *I* don't push him, then he'll have Doris barking at him at water aerobics for lagging behind the others."

"Then maybe you could talk to her, one professional to another," Lena suggested. "Tell her to take it easy."

"But the whole point of the class is to get in shape. I mean, if anyone is supposed to take it easy, look at me!"

"You're heartless," Wanda said.

Lena patted Fred and stood up. "It's because she's a physical therapist."

"It's true. They're a cruel lot," Wanda agreed.

"Excuse me, but that cuts me to the quick." Actually, Sarah's feelings were hurt. She might be cranky, but she cared so much about them. "Haven't you all seen marked improvement in your range of motion and strength?"

"Of course, dear," Lena assured her.

"Actually, my suggestion had nothing to do with my state. I was thinking of *you*," Hunt said.

Sarah frowned. "Me? You don't need to think about me."

"Au contraire. From what I observed last night, the end of the day is not the best time for you. You get extremely tired, am I right?"

"Ah-h," the other women cooed.

Sarah breathed in slowly. "You may be able to fool everyone else in this room, but you're not fooling me. Okay, today, I'll let you off easy."

"Easily," corrected Wanda.

Sarah turned and narrowed her eyes at her.

"Sorry, it's the high school teacher in me. Some things never die, especially the use of adverbs."

"I stand corrected," Sarah said, and then she leveled her gaze at Hunt. "Today I'll let you off easily, but don't count on it in the future."

"I bow to your good judgment," he said with an even broader smile. He turned and winked at the others. "Come, Fred. It's time to make the long trip home, even if it kills me."

Sarah walked over and opened the door. She held it open for him. "You'll be fine. It's all downhill on the way back."

Hunt waved goodbye, and Fred jerked on the leash, in hot pursuit of a squirrel scurrying across the parking lot.

Sarah winced as she closed the door. She turned

inside. "He'll be all right walking home, don't you think?"

Lena had once more picked up the copy of *Field and Stream* and didn't appear to hear. Sarah looked at Wanda. "He'll be fine, right?"

Wanda was coaxing Tiger back into her carryall. All the aggression appeared to have worn out the miniature fluff ball. "Don't worry about Fred, dear. He's a survivor."

Sarah didn't bother to clarify that she wasn't talking about the dog. She looked to Rosemary. As a military wife and mother of three grown sons, she always seemed to Sarah to demonstrate a great deal of common sense.

Only Rosemary was on the phone, talking to an insurance company.

"Oh, well, I suppose I can always call later. Not that it's really necessary."

Lena closed the magazine. She had a pensive look on her face. "Call?" she said, echoing Sarah's words. "Call whom? Huntington? He said he would call you. Which reminds me." She rummaged around in her bag and pulled out a Jitterbug cell phone. "I need to find out when Katarina and Ben and Matt are coming over for dinner."

Sarah didn't want to appear to be eavesdropping. "Well, whenever you're ready, I'll see you two ladies in the back." She turned toward the hall and heard her own cell phone ringing. She waddled back quickly to her office and retrieved her phone from her knapsack. She viewed the caller I.D. and smiled. "Yes? You and Fred got lost walking home?" she asked.

"Aw! I didn't know you cared," he joked.

"Frankly, I'm worried about Fred. You're just part of the package." There was a pause. "Listen, if you had plans tonight, I just want to say that you're under no obligation to pick me up. I wouldn't want to interfere."

"Actually, my reason for calling was that I've decided it's my turn to cook something after you made breakfast. Is there anything you don't eat?"

"Is there anything you *do* cook?"

"I can read, can't I? Anyway, you brought that enormous cookbook, so I figure there must be something in it that even I can cook."

"If you're sure?" She was dubious, but touched.

"As long as it explains how to boil water—no, I'm joking. Don't answer that."

Sarah laughed.

"Oh, my God!" he said.

She immediately straightened up. "What's wrong?"

"Nothing. I just realized that was the first time I've heard you laugh. It was nice. So what about dinner?"

Sarah felt her throat constrict. She pursed her lips. "Surprise me," she said.

CHAPTER FIFTEEN

LENA AND WANDA WALKED to the side of the tennis court after having lost the second set of their doubles match. It was almost noon, and the sun had played havoc with serving from their side of the court. They had split sets with the wife of the former dean of faculty and her daughter in town from California. Now a tiebreak would decide the outcome.

Wanda took a drink from her water bottle. "Can you believe she called that ball out? Maybe it's out in Palo Alto, but here in Grantham we call that in by a mile."

Lena toweled off her arm. Despite the cooler weather, she had built up a sweat running around the court. "I always say you can tell everything about a person by how they act on a tennis court. But never mind. We will take them in the tiebreak. We may be older, but we are smarter."

"You're right, I know. Let me just check on Tiger." Wanda opened her satchel farther. "Tiger, Tiger, how come you're so quiet? Come out and see Mommy."

When Tiger didn't peek his little black nose out of the bag, she reached in and lifted the dog out. He lay panting in her hands, barely able to lift his head.

Wanda turned worriedly to Lena. "Something's not right."

Lena stepped closer. "He doesn't look well at all. It wasn't too hot in the bag for him, was it?"

"Nonsense. He always stays in that bag." Wanda felt his chest. "Oh, no, his heart is racing. This isn't good." She turned to Lena, a sound of panic in her voice. "I don't know what I'd do if something happened to him."

Lena saw the anxious look in her friend's eyes and didn't waste any time. "Ladies," she called to their opponents, "we have an emergency here, a dog emergency. We'll have to resume play another time."

The mother and daughter walked to the net. "If you have to go, that's a forfeit, you know," the lanky daughter said. The tight-fitting stretch material of her Nike tennis dress showcased the budlike nipples of her high, firm breasts.

"What I know is, this is an emergency. We will resume play when I call. And then, after we beat you, you can share with us how you were downsized from Bank of America," Lena shot back. She was in no mood for know-it-all types who needed to learn a few manners.

She turned to Wanda. "Come. I'll drive you and Tiger right away to the vet. I'm sure there's something they can do."

It took less than ten minutes to get from the courts, across Route One to the veterinary office. Ten minutes of Wanda alternating between hugging Tiger fiercely to her chest or peering into his eyes for signs of distress.

"I've never seen him like this," Wanda worried. "They say that when an animal's listless, that's when you should worry. Do you think he's listless?"

She didn't wait for Lena to reply. "I've had him so

long. He's been through everything with me—those last years of teaching when all the administrators were concerned about was test scores, test scores, test scores—education went completely out the window. Of course, there was the breast cancer. I remember the way he just lay on the bed when I came home, never wanting to leave me alone. And now that I'm retired, he's my constant companion, giving me unquestioning love. Who am I going to speak to when I'm driving or at mealtime? He's the best sounding board I have—besides you, Lena."

The last was almost as an afterthought, but Lena didn't mind.

As soon as they arrived, the assistant at the front desk whisked Tiger into the back.

Lena sat on a built-in wooden bench in the reception area. Her arm was around Wanda, whose shoulders were hunched together.

"What if they can't do anything?" Wanda asked. She rocked back and forth. Her eyes never left the polished linoleum floor. "He's not a young dog, you know. Already eight years old."

"That's young for a dog. Why don't we just wait and see? The doctors are the best here," Lena comforted her. She glanced at the door to the examination room. This wasn't the first time she had sat waiting at a hospital. Almost fifty years ago as a young wife and mother, she had waited for news of her husband, Radek, who had collapsed on the street. The same chill traveled up the back of her neck. *But this isn't Radek,* she reminded herself and turned and patted Wanda reassuringly on her leg.

A little while later the doctor came out along with the

assistant. Both looked distressed. The young assistant was crying.

"Ms. Garrity? Tiger's owner?"

Wanda glanced up and rose. "Yes?"

Lena stood next to her.

The vet came over. "I am so sorry," she said. "We tried to do everything possible, but Tiger had a stroke. He showed indications of arterial fibrillation, an irregular heartbeat."

"But—but…I just brought him in for a checkup last week," Wanda protested. "He can't be dead." She started to cry.

"I know, I know. Sometimes, these things just happen. We tried to revive him, but he didn't respond. If you want to go back to visit him, he's on the table, and you're more than welcome to spend as much time as necessary."

Wanda started sobbing uncontrollably. She was beyond responding.

Lena put her arm around her. "Come. Let us say goodbye. It is very important." She guided Wanda toward the examination door. Then she saw the assistant raise her hand and stopped. "Yes?"

The young girl sniffled. She pulled a tissue from the pocket of her lab coat. "I know this is a bad time, but when Ms. Garrity is up to it, I need to know what she wants to do about the remains, payment, things like that. There's no rush," she said quietly to Lena.

Lena swallowed away her own tears—tears for Wanda's grief. The fact that Tiger had not been her favorite animal was beside the point. He had been a huge part of Wanda's life.

Lena turned her head so that only the assistant could hear. "I will take care of everything. But for now I need to help my friend."

CHAPTER SIXTEEN

"WHEN I SAID SURPRISE ME, I didn't mean give me less than thirty minutes' notice that I'd be eating at the Grantham Club!" Sarah said under her breath. "I didn't even have time to get back to my apartment, and I had to have Rosemary drive me to this dress shop in town called Tyrell's. I didn't even know there were still things like dress shops. And it was a miracle they had something with a drawstring waist. All in under fifteen minutes. I didn't dare look at the receipt. I'm sure the whole thing is way out of my budget."

Hunt put his hand under her arm and ushered her up the steps to the dining room. An institution among the well-to-do, the Grantham Club housed a dining room, a library, and several reception rooms on the ground floor. Upstairs were rooms for members, some of whom had occupied their quarters for more than forty years. For these gentlemen time hadn't changed, even if the club had been forced to admit women due to its aging membership, several Supreme Court decisions and financial necessity.

"Well, you look very nice." She did look very nice, Hunt thought. The plum-colored linen pants suit with its unstructured top looked highly sophisticated in its simplicity, and the color brought out the blue in her eyes. "And I like that scarf or whatever." He pointed at the long silk scarf casually draped around her neck and down the front of her top.

"Yes, apparently a local artist hand-painted it, inspired by a recent trip to China. They assured me I'd get a lot of wear out of it."

"Really, anyone would think you'd needed at least sixteen minutes, not just fifteen, to achieve the total effect."

Sarah halted once they'd reached the covered landing and cuffed him in the arm.

Hunt rubbed the spot through the sleeve of his blue blazer. "All kidding aside, I really want to apologize about putting you through all this. I had just finished putting together a *boeuf Bourguignon,* and it was starting to simmer when my mother called. By the way, do you know how many times I had to check Google for various cooking terms to figure out what to do? I'm still not sure how small to chop things up when the recipe says, 'mince finely.'"

"It just means tiny pieces." Sarah adjusted her scarf so that it hung the same length on either side.

"Anyway, there I was basking in my culinary glory—" Hunt didn't bother to go into the hours of sheer agony as he prepared the French stew "—when I get this call. She claimed she had left a message on my cell phone. I didn't bother to argue, even though I'm sure she really didn't. I tried to beg out of it, using you as an excuse."

"Oh, thanks. Just what I need—a bad start with your mother before she's even met me."

"Don't worry. My mother doesn't think badly of you. She doesn't think of you at all."

Sarah coughed. "And that's supposed to make me feel better?" She raised her hand and waved off her own comment. "Whatever. It's done. We're here." She faced Hunt and looked him over, unconsciously reaching up to adjust his orange-and-black rep tie—Grantham University colors. "There. You look very nice, too. If I didn't know better, I'd say your cheeks have filled out a little since this morning."

"I had another one of your muffins," he confessed.

"Good, that's what they're for. So, shall we face the music?" Sarah placed her hand against the small of her back and stretched.

Hunt noticed her cleavage peaking through the undone buttons of the top and he had renewed faith that all was right in the world.

He ushered her up a short flight of stairs and through the double French doors to the dining room. He didn't need the maitre d' to locate his mother. Iris always asked for the corner table by the window. Her back was toward the door, but he watched as the waiter leaned over and politely listened to her instructions. *Typical.* Hunt always felt his mother didn't so much converse as lecture.

Hunt turned to Sarah. "You know, there's still time to back out of this."

"Pardon me. Just because you don't want to see your mother doesn't mean you can use me as an excuse." She held up her hand. "So let's do this." She forged ahead in the direction of the maitre d'.

Hunt grabbed her by the elbow. "Hold it, Tonto, wrong direction." He guided her toward the far side of the high-ceilinged room. The large windows, which during the day brought in warming sunlight, were covered at night with heavy, striped drapes. Combined with the cream-colored walls, chair railings and old-fashioned wall sconces, the room bore more than a passing resemblance to Constitution Hall in Philadelphia. In fact, more than one signer of the Declaration of Independence had been a member of the Grantham Club, one of those being a Phox. Naturally.

Hunt maneuvered Sarah among the round tables set with white damask tablecloths, leaded crystal and hefty silverware. He nodded politely at several familiar faces, exchanged a few fleeting words and introduced Sarah, before reaching Iris.

"Mother, how nice to see you," he said, bending down to peck her cheek. Iris was one of those women of an undetermined age, and she had basically looked the same way, as far as Hunt could remember, his whole life. Other than letting her hair gradually go gray, she had always worn it in a rigorous upsweep, kept her figure rail thin, and her clothes tweedily appropriate. She wore her pearl earrings to the opera and while gardening.

Iris smiled briskly and patted the tablecloth next to her, indicating where she wanted him to sit. She raised her chin toward Sarah. "And you must be Sarah. Hunt has told me so much about you." She held out her hand, her discreetly jeweled Patek Philippe watch slipping decorously to the side of her wrist bone.

"Yes, Mother, may I present Sarah Halverson. Sarah, my mother, Iris Phox."

"I'm so pleased to meet you," Sarah said, shaking her hand. Her own large one dwarfed the older woman's. "I'm not sure what Hunt said about me, but as someone who's lived in the community for a number of years, your reputation of philanthropy is well-known."

"Thank you, dear. I try to do my part." Iris patted the place on her other side. "And why don't you sit over here.

In your condition, you need as much space as possible, am I right?"

Sarah looked under her eyebrows at Hunt, but dutifully moved to the chair. "Of course."

Hunt hurried around and held out her chair. "It's not as if we need to dock the family yacht, Mother." It was one thing for him to fend off his mother's glancing blows, but he didn't want Sarah to have to parry insensitive remarks all evening.

"That's all right," Sarah said, as if sensing the tension on his part. "In another week, I'll probably need a tugboat to ferry me around." She settled herself into her chair and picked up her menu. "This looks lovely. Is there something you recommend?"

"I always start with the consomme," Iris recommended, and when the waiter arrived a minute later with two martinis for Iris and Hunt, she proceeded to order for all three of them.

Iris raised her glass. "I already ordered us extra-dry martinis, Huntington, Beefeater's, of course."

"Of course," Hunt agreed with a wry smile.

"But I thought in your condition, water was more appropriate," she said to Sarah.

"Water's perfect." Sarah nodded and picked up her water glass. She took a sip.

"So, my son tells me you're planning on raising your baby on your own. The father is out of the picture?"

Sarah swallowed. "That's right." She took another fortifying sip.

"In my day, of course, that would have been unheard of. But you young women these days are different. How are your parents taking the news?"

Sarah coughed and patted her chest.

Hunt set down his martini—God, he now remembered why he never drank martinis. He looked across the table at Sarah, concerned, but she held up her hand to indicate she was all right, even as she coughed under her breath.

Hunt turned to Iris. A smile was still on his lips. "I think that Sarah is perfectly capable of raising her child the way she chooses. I don't think she needs to be cross-examined."

Sarah cleared her throat. "No, that's okay. Your mother was just asking the obvious. Mrs. Phox, as you can imagine, it was a bit of a shock for my parents in the beginning. They're fairly conservative, but I think that whatever their initial misgivings may have been, they are very supportive of me now. They know how much this baby means to me. And I think my mother is very eager about having a new grandchild."

Iris nodded. "I can imagine. Unfortunately, I haven't been blessed with any grandchildren." She smiled at Hunt.

He took another sip of his martini. At this point, he didn't care if he didn't like it or not.

"Of course in my day, it was only a certain type of girl who had a baby out of wedlock," Iris said.

"Mother!" This time when Hunt put down his drink, some of it sloshed over the ice cubes and onto the tablecloth. "I think you should apologize."

"Why, dear. I was merely making a historical and sociological observation." She lifted the breadbasket from the center of the table and offered it to Sarah. "A roll, or are you watching your weight?"

Sarah put her hand to her mouth. "Thank you, but no. I'll wait for the consomme."

Hunt reached across the table. "Well, I'll have a roll. With butter. Lots of butter." He ripped a roll in half and jabbed his butter knife at the tiny bowl of flower-shaped butter pats. He began spreading the soft roll. The butter was so cold it tore at the dough. He was furious.

It took a lot for Hunt to lose his cool. His mother had always had a way of being bluntly tactless, but in the past, he had brushed it off. Tonight, however, was different. Tonight the object of her remarks was Sarah. A protective instinct he had never known earlier came to the fore.

What had she done to deserve criticism? All she had done was tried to be a hardworking mother-to-be. She hadn't asked him for help. It had been more or less foisted upon her.

And, what's more, she was only here as a favor to him. She hadn't complained—okay, she had complained, but only in a reasonable way. And she had spent her own money on her new outfit, which looked very nice, indeed. As far as he was concerned, she could eat as many rolls as she wanted. She looked terrific, beautiful even. Yes, beautiful. And terrific. Inside and out.

He didn't like his mother's attitude. He didn't like it one bit. And it was going to stop. Right now. But getting his mother to get off her high horse was not a simple matter of telling her to stop. Iris was so self-absorbed she deflected criticism like a Teflon coating.

Still, Ben always claimed that Hunt had the ability to bargain with the best of them. It was his silver-tongued killer instinct that came out of nowhere and blindsided opponents. As Hunt knew, he wasn't his mother's son for nothing.

So instead of launching into a tirade against his

mother, he let the conversation drift through the soup
course, adding a *bon mot* or two here and there. The
tasteless cod and undercooked beans followed, and only
when his mother had finished the mound of potatoes
Dauphinois on her plate did he launch slyly into his
defense of Sarah.

"So, tell me, Mother. What did you want in life as a
young woman?" He leaned back and cocked his head.

Iris set her fork down on the plate. "Want? I'm not
sure I ever asked myself that question."

"Then what had you hoped for? Surely all young
girls have dreams—princessy-type things?" He waved
his hand in a spiral.

Iris patted her lips with her napkin. "I suppose I
hoped for what every woman of my generation wanted.
A successful marriage. Happy and healthy children."

Bingo! "Oh, dear," Hunt said in all sympathy. He
paused. "I guess, unfortunately, you struck out on both
accounts, didn't you?"

"Huntington, really, I don't really think this is the
type of conversation to have in public and in front of
strangers."

"This is a members-only club, and I hardly think
that any of them would dare breathe a word of criticism
about one of their most revered members. And Sarah
here is the soul of discretion."

Hunt leaned across the table and angled his head to
one side of the centerpiece of dahlias. "You see, my
parents' marriage was not exactly a match made in
heaven. For my mother," he said, twiddling his fingers,
"it was a case of a bun in the oven."

"Huntington, that's enough." Iris folded her napkin
neatly on her lap.

"I...ah...I don't think this is really any of my business," Sarah said quietly. She shifted in her chair.

Hunt waved off Sarah's objections. "Nonsense. It's so long ago, anyway. My father was summering in the Adirondacks when he met my mother. She was a waitress—"

"A hostess," Iris interrupted.

"Sorry, a hostess at a lodge where he was staying. My mother, though older than he, was quite attractive—"

"She still is," Sarah said.

Iris ran a hand down her throat, her fingers lingered on the double strand of yellow pearls. "Thank you, Sarah."

"What can I say? My father was smitten. Because, you see, not only did my father, Huntington Phox III, pluck my mother out of the obscurity of upstate New York, allowing her to wave goodbye forever to her modest past as a shop owner's daughter—"

"My father ran a gas station, a very respectable gas station."

"Yes, of course. He was in oil," Hunt joked.

No one at the table laughed.

"My father took her away from all that, but not out of love and devotion, but because decorum forced him to. That, and my imminent arrival. No matter, my mother achieved her goal—she was transported to Grantham to become the dutiful member of a prominent family, and my father fulfilled his obligations—he provided an heir to carry on the family name. Unfortunately, my father also liked to carry on in his own way. He wasn't quite so sterling, was he, Mother?"

"There's no need to speak ill of the dead."

"I'm not speaking ill, merely speaking the truth.

Because you see, it wasn't long before my father essentially moved out of the house for a convenient little *pied-à-terre* in Manhattan, close to his white-shoe law firm and a string of willing secretaries."

"His decision was one of convenience," Iris argued. She held her hand up when she saw the waiter approach. "We'll just have coffee, Joseph," she said. "Decaf?" She looked at Sarah.

"Yes, please," Sarah said. She pressed her hand to her stomach.

Hunt watched as the plates were removed. "And I'll have a cognac, too, please," he said.

Iris cleared her throat.

Hunt ignored the warning. "Let's see, where were we? Oh, yes, my father. Not a nice young man, it turned out. But we'll never know if he would have reformed or remained a reprobate, because he died after being hit by a bus, of all things."

Iris stared at her son. "I suppose there is a point to this story?"

"Point? I guess it's that things were done a certain way in your time, and things are different now. *Ergo,* I really don't think you should be judging Sarah the way you did."

"I'm sorry, Huntington, but some things are right, and some things are not," Iris fired back. Her overbite became more pronounced.

Hunt's anger flared to a new level. How could she be so unfeeling, so cold?

Unhappily, he could feel the same ice in his own heart, and he called on it as he spoke slowly and carefully. "The second part of your dream—to have a happy and healthy child didn't work out, either, did it?"

Hunt narrowed his eyes and continued in a low, almost menacing voice. "Because you couldn't prevent your so-called golden boy from committing the one crime you can't deal with. He got cancer."

"But that's a thing of the past now, Huntington. You should leave it behind, move on." Iris sat up even straighter.

"See—" he looked at Sarah "—she can't even say the word. *Cancer,* mother. C-A-N-C-E-R. The Big C. You see, no one in our family gets a cold, let alone has cancer. The Phoxes are too strong a stock. It takes a Broadway bus to level them. Sickness is a sign of weakness, and we can't have that. Not when we're too busy holding up ourselves to the community as the paragons of perfection."

Hunt turned his glare away from Iris and addressed Sarah's shocked expression. He tried to soften his tone. "You see, my mother's way of dealing with my little 'problem,' was to bury herself in good works. True she agreed to see the oncologist after the initial diagnosis, but thereafter she refused to acknowledge or accept my trips to New York for treatments."

"You always maintained you could deal with that yourself," Iris protested. The coffee had arrived, and she placed both hands on her cup. They shook.

"You could have insisted. Never mind." He waved away his own suggestion. He knocked back one sip of cognac, then pushed the snifter away. He'd never used alcohol as a way of drowning his emotions, and he wasn't about to start now.

Instead, he laughed, an ironic, amused chuckle. One that he had practiced on many other occasions. He looked past the table to an oil painting on the wall, only vaguely registering a pedestrian landscape. "I'd go into the city, sit for hours in a chair while poison dripped into my arm, and then stay overnight at a hotel to recover. Then I'd take the train back the next day and drag myself to work, just as if nothing had happened. I spared you and everyone else the embarrassment of seeing me puke in the toilet. I won't even go into the diarrhea. It is the dinner table after all. And the fact that all my hair fell out, needless to say was never discussed."

"Why bring it up and embarrass you?" Iris determinedly sipped her coffee.

"Mother, I think it was so obvious!"

Iris signaled to the waiter to bring the check.

"How disappointing, therefore, it must be for you to have a son like me." His anger was gone, replaced by sadness.

The waiter silently returned with the bill, and Iris eyed the items.

"Please, I'd like to pay for the meal," Sarah offered. "It's the least I can do for your invitation."

Iris patted her hand. "That's really very sweet, Sarah. I'm sure you are a well brought-up woman and will make a fine mother. But it just goes on my monthly bill, anyway, and it is my pleasure to have met you."

Iris signed with a flourish, then looked sideways at her son. "I'm not sure what inspired this outburst, Huntington, but if you meant to hurt me, you have succeeded. Still, you are my son, and I love you dearly. However—"

She held her hand up when he was about to speak. "You may criticize me, but in my defense, allow me to point out that I have a sense of purpose. You may not agree with what I think is important, you may ridicule the way I act and the values I have, but what exactly are you doing to contribute to society? I saw Rufus Tread-way at the town Planning Board meeting for the new hospital construction, and I gather that even your dog is without a modicum of social behavior."

"He's a puppy, and besides, Sarah and I plan to take him to Rufus's dog obedience class this Sunday."

Iris started to push her chair back from the table to rise. Hunt, well schooled, rose and held her chair.

"Wait a minute, since when did I become a part of this project?" Sarah asked, getting up slowly.

Iris marched away from the table. Hunt and Sarah trailed behind.

"As my roommate I was sure you'd want to partici-pate in training a fellow member of the household," Hunt whispered.

Sarah shook her head. "Some household."

At the cloakroom, he helped his mother on with her wool coat and they exchanged small talk as she pulled her leather gloves on. She waited for a small peck on the cheek before bidding them goodbye with all decorum and as if nothing remarkable had passed at dinner. She even mentioned to Sarah that she would like to invite her to her next Women's Club luncheon.

"We have invited speakers on such topics as historic preservation and colonial gardening techniques," Iris said.

"I'm not sure it will fit into my work schedule, but thank you so much for thinking of me," Sarah replied.

After Iris left in her black Mercedes, Sarah walked silently across the club parking lot to the car, her hands fisted by her sides.

"You were wonderful. Why don't we just forget

about what happened tonight?" Hunt beeped open the Porsche.

"Just get me home," she said, sliding into the seat. She huffed as she drew the seat belt across her chest.

"I know. It was terrible." Hunt started the car.

"Yes, but I also need to pee. Desperately."

They sat in silence all the way home, both alone with their thoughts. They waited in the car as the garage door lifted. Hunt pulled the car into the space, then came around to open her door. He waited for her to get out.

Sarah sat there, looking straight ahead, not moving. "Wait a minute," she said, staring at the dashboard.

"I thought you said you need to go to the bathroom?" He rested his hand on the open door.

"I do, but this is important. What you said back there about just forgetting this? I can't, and you shouldn't, either." She rubbed her forehead. "I don't like saying this, but I have to. I hated you tonight. You were mean and hurtful to your mother." For the first time, she glanced up at Hunt.

"She deserved it. What kind of a mother never shows a modicum of emotion to her child and whose idea of a little get-together is the formal setting of the Grantham Club? That's where you take a client for lunch, not a place to catch up with your son."

"It doesn't matter. She's your mother. My mother drives me crazy, too, and I can be mean to her, but, frankly, even at my worst I am nothing like the way you behaved." She huffed and puffed and eased her legs to the side and out of the door. "Here, help me up?" She raised an arm.

He guided her up and held on to her as she became vertical. "Hold still. Get your bearings," he warned.

"Yes, Mother," she cracked. "You can let go now."

"In a minute." He didn't budge and instead replayed the evening in his mind. "You know, maybe the truth is I am like my father, charming on the outside, mean on the inside?"

Sarah shook her head. "You're nothing like your father."

"How do you know? We've only just met."

"Will you get my knapsack and work clothes out of the back?"

"You're steady?"

She nodded. "If you were like your father, we wouldn't even be having this conversation. Someone like your father never would have bothered to be a good son. Never would have taken in a stray dog. Never would have taken in a stray like me, for that matter."

He pressed the passenger seat forward and reached in the back. "Well, maybe I'm not a louse, but I was very upset. I mean, when she started to say those hurtful things to you about 'certain kind of women,' I just lost it."

Sarah patted him on his cheek. "That's sweet. But really, I don't need a knight in shining armor. Besides, that comment may have made you angry, but I don't think that's why you were so upset."

"No? I don't even have the excuse of wanting to come to your rescue?" He scrunched up his brow and batted his eyelashes.

She smiled. "You look as pathetic as Fred when you make that face. Speaking of which, he must be going crazy inside."

He was immensely relieved to see her smile. He'd take on his mother anytime for her, even if she didn't need a protector. He grabbed her hand when she drew it away. "So tell me. If you weren't the real cause of my outburst, what was?"

Sarah wet her lips. "You're upset about getting cancer because you don't think it was fair."

"You're damn straight I'm upset. How come I got cancer and not some lousy wife-beater or deadbeat father? What did I ever do to deserve it?"

"Nobody deserves to get cancer. Sometimes things just happen that we have no control over."

Hunt was quiet for a moment. "I guess I wanted everyone else to feel as miserable as me."

"Well, I think you managed that tonight."

Hunt shook his head. "You're right. I was awful. Mean, spiteful. My behavior was uncalled for."

"Totally. But probably inevitable."

"How do you mean?"

"All I'm saying is, maybe it was finally time for you to break out of that emotionally cool cocoon you live in? Maybe you needed to get angry the way you did? Because maybe you finally decided to stop wearing that mask of laid-back insouciance and started feeling something real."

"Insouciance?"

She poked him in the arm. "Stop it! That's just what I'm talking about. I think this whole confrontation was a long time coming, and you finally let your guard down enough to admit that you're angry—angry at your mother, angry at the world, but most of all angry at yourself because you got cancer."

"So now I suppose you're going to say, 'Get over it'?"

"No, I was going to say that I think it would be a good

idea if first thing tomorrow morning you had flowers delivered to your mother. Lots of them."

"You think flowers, even a whole florist shop's worth will be enough?"

"No, but it's a start."

From inside the house, there was the sound of scratching.

Sarah looked around him. "Fred."

"He can wait a minute." Hunt looked down at her, at her fine blond hair falling to her shoulders, and her small upturned nose, her full lips, her amazing eyes full of intelligence and insight. "I think there's one more thing I need to do."

And he bent down and kissed her hard and fast on the lips, a thank-you kiss and more. Much more for him, Hunt felt as he rocked back unsteadily on his feet.

Sarah seemed to wobble a little, too. She gripped the top of the car. She caught her breath. "Okay, that's different."

"Different good?" he asked.

"Different, I have to think about it. And now, move—before I do something really embarrassing."

CHAPTER SEVENTEEN

"SARAH, HUNT, IT'S GOOD to see you made it," Rufus greeted them as they walked through the swinging doors into the high school gymnasium. "And, Fred, good dog." He pulled out a piece of hot dog from a fanny pack and coaxed the dog over. Fred slunk low to the floor, but timidly moved forward when he got a whiff of the treat. "Good dog. You're not so afraid today." Rufus offered him another treat, and Fred took it much more readily.

"Okay, folks." Rufus turned and addressed the class members. "There're some stools to sit on while we wait for everyone. It looks like we still have another couple and their dog to come. In the meantime, why don't we all introduce ourselves and our dogs? So, to start, I'm Rufus Treadway, and I'm here to guide you and your pets in the Beginner Dog Obedience Class."

Sarah and Hunt sat on the first two low stools against the cinderblock wall. Banners hung from above declaring Grantham High School the Class B Girls Basketball Champions for four years running. Fred was not nearly so enthusiastic, trying futilely to hide between Sarah and Hunt.

Sarah introduced herself, as did Hunt. They tried to coax Fred out from his hiding place to greet his fellow students, but he was intent on facing the wall. She patted him encouragingly. "He's shy with new people," she said apologetically.

"Fred's a shelter dog and needs time and patience." Rufus said encouragingly. "Did you bring some pieces of string cheese like I suggested? Food can be a great stress reliever. Next?" He looked to the woman seated beyond Hunt.

That was Marjorie with her dog, Sally, a nine-month-old black Lab who loved everyone. Then there were Rick and Jenny. They came with their Rottweiler, Bessie, who had a tendency to lunge when anyone got near. The Quigley family had turned out en masse with their one-year-old Saint Bernard, Tommy. Tommy was very good at drooling and being a large rug. They explained that he also liked to eat remote controls.

Just when all the introductions were winding up, Carleton and Anna—pronounced, "Ah-n-na"—walked in with a four-year-old poodle named Toulouse—pronounced "Two-lose." Toulouse said hello by yipping at all the dogs and straining on the leash, but when Carleton took a seat on one of the stools, his pressed jeans rising to reveal well-polished cowboy boots, Toulouse sat obediently by his side.

"That's not fair," Hunt whispered to Sarah. "Toulouse is showing off. He already knows how to sit."

Sarah patted Fred reassuringly. "Don't worry," she said to Hunt out of the side of her mouth. "Fred may not know how to sit, but he would never think of yapping."

Rufus started passing around loose-leaf binders. "Here are some folders for everyone. You can use them to keep the summaries of what we did in class as well as the homework assignments I'll give you at the end of each class. If you open them up now, you'll see I've included ten tips for preventing behavioral problems."

Hunt skimmed them over. "'Set rules right away and stick to them. Avoid situations that can stimulate bad behavior. Observe your pet and provide the necessary care.'"

Sarah read over his shoulder and nodded. "I like number six. 'Don't encourage aggressive play or biting.' You'd never bite aggressively, would you, Fred?"

Fred seemed to take courage from her words because he ventured forth with his nose, resting it in Hunt's crotch.

"The philosophy of this class is positive reinforcement," Rufus explained. "By that I mean rewarding your dog for doing something right rather than punishing him for doing something wrong."

"I promise to reward you when you burp the baby," Hunt murmured.

Sarah wet her lips. "You'll come see the baby?"

"When your dog does something naughty, he's trying to get your attention. Any kind of response, negative or positive, tells the dog that that kind of behavior gets your attention. What we want to do is put you in charge of your dog, set boundaries where you and he can interact confidently and allow you to enjoy living together." Rufus walked casually among the group as he spoke.

"Now I want each of you to stand up. We are going to start with getting your dog to listen to you," Rufus instructed. "The command is 'watch me.' You look at your dog, say the command, and when he does, you reward your dog with a treat and praise. If your dog doesn't respond to your voice, put a treat in front of your nose to get his attention. Then repeat the command.

Why don't I demonstrate with Sally here." He walked over to the playful Labrador. Naturally, when Rufus held her leash taut above her head and said the words, Sally responded like a pro.

Hunt looked reassuringly at Fred. "Don't worry, Fred, you'll get the hang of this. If I can learn to fox-trot, you can master 'watch me.'"

"Just keep the string cheese coming," Sarah advised.

"I'm sure that would have helped with the dance lessons, too," he said.

"Okay, let's have everybody spread out and work on 'watch me,' and don't forget to reward your dog when she responds."

"Here, let me go first. Then I'll help you up," Hunt suggested to Sarah. He stood up, forgetting that the plastic bag of treats was on his lap. They promptly fell to the floor.

"You're a failure already," Sarah said drily.

Hunt made a face and leaned over to pick up the bag.

Toulouse spotted the cheese and pounced, clipping Hunt on the cheek with a nail. He eased Toulouse away with the back of his hand and stood up.

Ah-n-na rushed over. "Oh, are you all right?"

"It's fine. Just a scratch," Hunt said.

"I think she means the dog," Sarah said to him.

After that, the class went quickly as everyone tried to master the exercises. Finally, Rufus spoke up.

"That's enough for today. Your dog is tired because he's had to use his mind. That's both rewarding and exhausting. Here's the sheet reviewing what we learned from this class. Remember, work on what we've done all through the week, using positive reinforcement and marking each time your dog responds, teaching him that he's doing the right thing. Next week, we'll move on to loose-leash walking and 'sit.'"

Hunt and Sarah gathered up all the dog paraphernalia and Fred. For once, the dog wasn't pulling as they walked out. "Fred did great, don't you think? Much better than that poodle," Hunt said.

Sarah waited for the automatic doors to open and read the behavior tip sheet again. "Maybe I should get this laminated and put it up over the baby's crib? Frankly, I need all the help I can get since I know just about nothing about babies, let alone bringing up kids."

"What do you mean? You were raised on a farm. I thought things like birth and babies and tiny little feet running around were as natural as churning butter."

"Excuse me, I grew up on a farm, not a commune. And we had machines to milk the cows. I did not sit around pulling on teats. As to taking care of kids, I was the baby in the family. Everybody else looked after me. By the time my brothers had children of their own, I had already gone to New York. And where I was living in Queens, nobody had kids."

Hunt let Fred take a weary pee on a sycamore tree before they crossed the street to his parked car. He angled the driver's seat forward so that Fred could hop in the back. The dog was so tired he stumbled over the seat belt.

Sarah circled the car to get to the passenger seat and bent down to open the door. "You know, this car seems lower and lower to me every day."

Hunt came around and held open her door until she lowered herself in. He watched her struggle as she tried to swivel around to get the seat belt. "Here, let me get it."

"Thank you." Sarah watched him pull it out as far as it could go. He reached across her, his arm resting lightly on her stomach, and was locking it in place when she grabbed his arm.

"What? Is something wrong?" he asked, worry in his voice.

She shook her head. "I was just thinking. Don't… don't tell anyone I said that—about not knowing anything about babies. They might get the impression that I can't handle the whole being-a-single-mom thing."

Hunt studied her face. "Your secret is safe with me." He smiled. Suddenly he switched his focus to her belly. "Hey, was that the baby? I felt something."

Sarah placed her hand on her stomach. "Yeah, he seemed to have enjoyed the obedience class, too. Here…" She picked up his hand and moved it to the left. "Can you feel? He's really kicking up a storm."

"So you know it's a boy?" He moved his hand more to the center as the baby shifted inside her.

"No, I told the ultrasound technician not to tell me. I wanted it to be a secret." She looked down at her stomach and Hunt's hand resting atop, his face aglow as he followed the baby's movements. It all seemed so right, so meant to be. It would be so easy to pretend that they were a couple, bringing their dog to class and now going home to read the newspaper together, have some tea, maybe take a nap….

Sarah looked away. Who was she kidding? They weren't a couple. "I think he's stopped moving now," she said.

"Oh, yeah." Hunt seemed reluctant to remove his hand. "But that was something. Thanks."

She could tell from his tone that he wanted her to look at him, but Sarah refused. She kept her eyes focused on the blank wall of the high school.

Hunt came around and started up the car. They drove for a block in silence, coming to a halt at the stop sign by the Choir College. Across the street was a memorial garden for a former Grantham mayor, the purples and pinks of fall mums recalling her favorite colors. Hunt turned to her as he waited to proceed through the intersection.

"So, tell me, have you made any arrangements for child care?"

Sarah looked around. "I think you can go now," she said.

He put the car in gear. "I'm sorry. I didn't mean to pry."

Sarah breathed in slowly and rested her head against the headrest. "No, it's a fair question. I've got a six-week maternity leave from work. When I go back, Katarina's housekeeper, Amada, has already offered to help out three days a week."

"That still leaves two not covered." Hunt waited at the traffic light on Main Street.

"Yeah, I know. I've already started to look into day care, but on my salary the places that I liked the most are kind of out of my reach, which, truthfully, does have me a bit worried."

She stared at Hunt. "And don't tell anyone that, either, especially Katarina and Julie. And Lena and Wanda. If they found out, the whole town would know. So, you've got to promise. You, too, Fred." She glanced over her shoulder. The dog was fast asleep, curled up like a tight little fuzzy doughnut.

Hunt turned into the side street beside his house. Sarah, on wordless cue, removed the automatic garage door opener from the glove box. He waited as the door rumbled open. "Don't worry. Our lips are sealed, but that still doesn't mean I can't help out. I'm happy to, you know."

"I know. Thanks." She nodded and tears welled in her eyes.

Hunt pulled on the hand brake. "What's the matter?" He put his hand under her chin to raise her face.

Sarah sniffed. "Hey, you're stopped in the middle of the street. Aren't you worried you might block someone wanting to get by?"

"Let them figure it out." Her turned her head to face him. "Let me propose something radical."

Her heartbeat picked up.

"Why not move in with me for a while—after the baby's born? I mean, I'm still getting back on my feet, trying to figure out what to do with the rest of my life. You're still up in the air about how to take care of the baby. If you're here, I can help out, at least until you're more settled. I don't see any reason why not to. After all, you're not attached. I'm not attached. It's not as if I'm talking about a long-term commitment."

No, he wasn't, was he? Sarah thought to herself. Was she disappointed? In a way, yes. But those thoughts were just a fantasy—not reality. Not everyday life. Everyday life required admitting you were just like everybody else, not that different from your family back in Minnesota. That you needed to make compromises, make do, take joy in small things.

"Let me think about it," she said. She knew what he suggested made logical sense. But deep inside she still wanted to hold on to her privacy and independence, while at the same time dreaming of something bigger....

Hunt shifted in his seat. "Well, while you're thinking about it, think about this, too." He cupped the side of her head and brought her face close to his. And then he kissed her, starting lightly but quickly easing apart her lips to explore and share. Sarah felt herself responding immediately to the tastes, the feel, the giving that passed from his lips to hers.

Until he finally pulled back. "In case you're interested, that wasn't part of my social rehabilitation," he said. There was a satisfied smile on his lips.

Sarah could just imagine what her lips looked like. She shook her head, astonished. *This couldn't be happening, could it?* "In case you haven't noticed, I'm pregnant," she said in an attempt to de-mystify the moment.

"As far as I know neither lymphoma nor chemo has done anything to diminish my eyesight."

"But I mean, you don't really find that attractive, do you? I mean, look! I'm as big as a mountain!"

He studied her through narrowed eyes. "Interesting about that. There's no denying that you're an attractive woman. And somehow, your being pregnant now, only makes you more womanly, ergo more sexy."

"But what about the fact that this is someone else's baby?"

He frowned in thought. "Frankly, I don't see that as a problem. Say you'd been married before and already had a kid. Would I reject him out of hand? Of course not."

She looked at him baffled. "You're weird, you know that?"

"It's part of my charm. So tell me you'll at least think about my offer?"

She rubbed her mouth. Her lips were definitely swollen. She nodded, bobbing her head. "No guarantees, though."

"Are there ever any?" He turned and released the emergency brake. "I don't know about you, but I'm feeling pretty chipper at the moment. So good in fact, that I'm thinking of calling up Ben and Katarina and inviting them for dinner at our place. I still have the *boeuf Bourguignon* in the fridge, you know."

"I know." She had lifted the lid on the stew that morning. There was enough to feed all of central New Jersey. "Can we at least wait until Fred has learned 'sit'?" But two words resonated in her mind—*our place.*

CHAPTER EIGHTEEN

"SWITCH," LENA SHOUTED to Wanda as she crossed from the deuce to the ad side of the tennis court. It was the resumption of their suspended match with the mother and grown daughter. Normally, Lena knew how Wanda took particular delight in thrashing a player who was a good thirty years younger than she. But since Tiger had died, not much had been normal for her.

Lena, of course, was much too mature to relish beating people simply because they were younger and fitter. She liked beating anyone, period.

"I got it," Wanda called out. She backpedaled for a lob, her left foot crossing over her right. A light breeze caused the ball to drift farther back than she anticipated. The frame of her racket tipped the ball, and the ball ricocheted. And the outside edge of her right tennis shoe slipped on the court at an awkward angle. She cried out, falling to the ground. She clutched her ankle.

Lena came running. "Wanda, are you all right?"

Wanda looked up and frowned as their opponents came from the other side of the court. "They're here to inspect the damage," she said under her breath.

"Stop it," Lena chastised. "They're just concerned." Lena looked over and explained the situation. "I think it's just a little sprain," she said. "But we really do intend to finish this match."

The out-of-work banker daughter, who had previously been so snippy, held her tongue.

"Good then," Lena said when she didn't get any complaints. "Next week it is, right, Wanda?"

Wanda screwed up her face in pain. "This is so irritating. We were just about to break them, and we could have taken the first set." She swatted Lena away when she put her hand under her elbow to help her up. Instead, she rolled to her left side, braced herself on the butt of her racket, and hoisted herself up. She hopped to the chairs at the side of the court.

"There are other things besides winning," Lena said, following her.

"So you say. Given my age and current single status, sex is not on the horizon. That leaves only death and taxes. For joy, for joy."

The mother and daughter cooed their "get well soon's" and packed up their gear.

Wanda barely acknowledged their sympathies. "That's all I need. Another injury. First my elbow, now my ankle. I'm falling apart in front of my eyes, and I don't have Tiger to help me get through it. I made him promise to live a long life, and look what happened?" she grumbled.

"C'mon," Lena said. "We will go and get some cold on it right away. I have a bag of frozen peas in the freezer just for such an occasion. I think Katarina even left an Ace bandage in the bathroom vanity from when she was living with me last year. If it's not there, I can always call her."

"Watch! It won't be Katarina we're going to need to call. It'll be Sarah."

"You don't need Sarah," Lena hushed her. "She has enough on her mind."

"You mean the appointment with Julie this morning? From the way she apologized for canceling our PT session, you would have thought she was cutting me off without bread and water."

"I know. She's too conscientious for her own good. I texted Hunt, and he promised to let me know if there were any complications about those fainting spells of hers."

Wanda reached around and slipped her warm-up jacket off the back of the chair. Then she picked up her tennis racket and worked it into her bag. There was no yapping from Tiger to greet her or to complain about being crowded. Wanda sighed.

"I suppose it's good that Hunt went with her. I know I said she's a strong and capable woman, but in moments of stress, especially at the doctor's office, it's nice to have another set of ears. Remember how you used to come with me to see the surgeon after I found out I had breast cancer?" She sniffed.

"Of course I came with you. What are friends for?" She stood to the side, holding herself back when Wanda got to her feet. That didn't stop her from grabbing Wanda's bag and walking slowly next to her as she hobbled to her car.

Lena pursed her mouth. She didn't like this attitude she was seeing from Wanda. Something wasn't right. She waited until they got to the cars, and when Wanda was about to open her car door, she looked her in the eye. "What are you really talking about, Wanda? I know you went for a mammogram appointment last week.

Did your breast cancer come back again and you're not telling me?"

Wanda shook her head. "I won't get the results until next week, but, no, I'm not worried. I'm sure everything is fine."

A squirrel ran across the grass and jumped down the steps by the courts. He snickered as he raced up a Norway maple.

Wanda watched him disappear. She turned back to Lena. "I know you said next week for tennis, but I'm not so sure."

"What do you mean you're not so sure? It's a little sprain. You act like it's the end of the world. What's going on?"

"I'm merely being realistic. At my age, you just don't bounce back from injuries, no matter how seemingly minor."

"What do you mean at your age? You're two years younger than I am, and you don't see me slowing down."

Wanda shrugged her shoulders. "Okay, so maybe I *am* a little nervous about the mammogram. But once you've had cancer, no matter what, it's always in the back of your mind. And to tell you the truth, I'm not sure I can go through it again."

"Wanda." Lena touched the sleeve of her friend's warm-up outfit—black with rhinestones, typical Wanda. "If the news turns out to be bad, you and I, we will get through this again. You are a strong woman. The strongest I know."

Wanda held up her hand. "Not anymore. Not since Tiger died."

Lena said a silent, *aha*. She rubbed Wanda's shoulder in comfort. "I know how much he meant to you."

"People who don't have dogs can't begin to imagine the loss," Wanda said.

"Maybe. But I can identify with the death of a dear one." Her husband, Radek, might be dead for more than fifty years, but there were times when she still got a catch in her throat—on the date of their anniversary, on the birth of their grandchild, when the sun shone a certain way over the snow crystals and made the world sparkle like a Fabergé egg. But now was not her time to grieve.

"You can get another dog, Wanda," she suggested.

"No, I couldn't take breaking in a new dog. And I certainly couldn't take having another one die on me. It would be too much. In fact, everything is too much for me these days." Wanda looked at her friend with an expression of exhaustion. "These days I even find owning a house too much. The mortgage payments alone—they're too much, especially on my fixed income! I was a public schoolteacher not John D. Rockefeller."

"But your house is fairly new compared to mine," Lena said. Lena's modest clapboard home, like the other houses on her tree-lined street, dated back to the nineteenth century. Newly arrived yuppies to Grantham were rediscovering the street's architectural funkiness and convenient proximity to the coffee shops, specialty stores and neighborhood restaurants.

Wanda, on the other hand, lived in a sixties development of modest split-levels near the shopping center. She had a garage and a bay window, but none of the charm of Lena's place.

"Nobody wants a place like that anymore," Wanda

said, stating what they both knew. "You know that house that finally sold on my street a few months ago? It went for forty thousand below the asking price. And now the new owners are tearing it down to build some McMansion."

She sighed again. "Besides, any house requires work, and I'm just not up to it anymore. I hate getting ripped off by workmen who see this little old lady and immediately get dollar signs in front of their eyes." She mimicked her words with her hands in front of her face. "I'm not like you. You've always been handy. I wouldn't know how to use a screwdriver if you told me which end was which." Wanda turned to open the back door of her Maxima. "Here. Give me my bag."

Lena watched Wanda stow her case. "Okay, I understand what you are saying, but what does using a screwdriver have to do with cancer?"

Wanda frowned and held up her hands beseechingly. "Nothing. And everything. The bottom line is everything is falling apart—my body, my house. And all of it takes money and time to fix—two things I don't have a lot of in the long run. I know, I know, you say you'll help, and you've always been a great friend. But now you have Katarina living in town. And Ben and Matt. Pretty soon, who knows, you'll have a great-grandchild. My God, just saying that makes me feel ancient."

"If you feel ancient, how about me?" Lena asked, still trying to buck up her friend even though she realized it was going to take more than a bit of kidding around.

"At least you are growing older with a family. All the time I was teaching, my students were my family. What can I say? I read *The Prime of Miss Jean Brodie* at an impressionable age."

"From this Brodie lady I know nothing. But I do know how much you influenced your students. Look how many still send you Christmas cards and announcements when they have children."

"But have I ever been able to send someone a photo of me holding a tiny baby? And don't say my nephews, because as we all know they were never tiny bundles of joy."

"It's true. It's a good thing they live in San Antonio. It would be even better if they moved to Guam," Lena agreed.

"And now I don't even have Tiger to be near me." Wanda bit back tears.

"You'll be getting his ashes in a few weeks—in a beautiful cedar box, and I think we should say goodbye to him in style. We'll have a lovely ceremony and spread his ashes wherever you want. We could even spread them here at the tennis courts. He always liked sitting by the picnic table."

Wanda looked fondly at the table next to the court. Dogs were strictly prohibited from the courts, which hadn't stopped Wanda or Tiger. "He did, didn't he?"

Lena breathed in, though not entirely easily. Finding a suitable resting place for Tiger was a relatively simple problem. Rescuing Wanda was another entirely.

CHAPTER NINETEEN

"OKAY, YOU CAN TAKE YOUR FEET down from the stir-rups now." Julie rolled her stool away, stripped off her rubber gloves and threw them in the medical-waste bin. "Everything appears just the way it should. I don't think we need to do anything further for now. You say the fainting spells have leveled off?"

Sarah swung her legs to the side and rolled to a sitting position. The paper gown she'd put on for the exam was woefully insufficient. "I've felt a little-light headed once or twice but nothing serious, especially now that I'm following your advice on snacking and all that stuff."

"You're still going to the water aerobics class?" Julie wrote notes while she questioned Sarah.

"The second class meets tomorrow night, and I was planning on going—with Hunt."

"Well, I want you to be careful. If you feel at all faint, out of the water—pronto." She looked up from her clipboard. "And how are things with Mr. Hunt? You know, I still remember him from high school. He was two years ahead of me and was this golden god. How the mighty have fallen."

Sarah frowned at Julie's tone. "Hunt's doing pretty well, considering the chemo treatment, not to mention lymphoma." She ignored the raised eyebrows from Julie.

"Can I get dressed? Because if I weren't monumentally pregnant right now, I'd be totally freezing."

"Oh, yeah, you can put your clothes on. Then we'll have a talk in my office next door." She stood up and walked to the door. And stopped. "Lymphoma, huh? I figured something like that from the evidence of the chemo treatment. What type?"

"Hodgkin's."

"As cancers go, that's a good one."

"It seems his prognosis is good, but at the same time, it's easy for us to say. If you're going through it, I'm sure it's not that reassuring—like telling someone they're only a little bit pregnant."

"You're right. Anyway, the way I look at it, if he can survive his mother—who has been very generous to the hospital, I must confess—he can survive anything." She turned. "I'll just wait outside while you get dressed."

Sarah rolled off the table and reached for her clothes. She slipped on her underpants and her leggings. The elastic waistband had stretched to twice its original size. The only thing more gigantic was the ugly white bra she was just about to put on, her cup size having risen liked activated yeast. She gave up trying to do the hooks behind her and swung the bra around to the front to do up the fastners.

Julie's comment about Hunt's mother came back to haunt her. She stared down at her belly. "You think I'll be a good mother? What if I don't love you? Who's to say I will? There're no guarantees, you know, that some mysterious spark will be there, that an instant bond will form."

She shrugged, but her anxieties remained even as she finished dressing. She picked up her knapsack and opened the door, ready to walk down the hall with Julie. But she was talking on her cell, so Sarah headed for the office alone. And practically stumbled over Hunt.

He was sitting in one of two chairs facing Julie's desk and stood as soon as he saw her. "So are you all right? No complications?"

"Hunt, didn't I tell you that you could stay in the waiting room, and that I'd tell you all about it?"

"Naomi the office manager was so nice. She told me I could come in for the consultation after the exam," Hunt said.

Sarah shook her head, but she let him stay.

"So?" He straightened the chair for Sarah to sit. "What's the verdict?"

Julie marched in, took one look at Hunt and har-rumphed. "Well, this is a surprise."

"As soon as I came into the reception area, I could tell immediately this was your office," Hunt said, seemingly oblivious to Julie's skepticism. "It was all the needle-point pillows. Sarah's shown me some that you made for her, too. You know, my mother would love your work—all those intricate stitches. Maybe you could give a talk at her club some time?"

Sarah patted his hand and looked over to Julie, who for once had no quick rejoinder. "So, should we tell him, doctor, that I am expecting?"

He glanced at Julie. "And here she told me it was heartburn." Hunt turned serious. "Really, she's okay, right?"

Julie fussed with the paper clip that held together the top sheets of Sarah's file, and then finally, she cleared her throat and looked up.

"As I told Sarah in the examining room, everything

appears to be normal for someone in her thirty-first week of pregnancy. Now that you're being more careful, the fainting seems to have abated—not that I'm giving you license to drive again, you understand." She gave them both a cold eye and only eased off when they murmured agreement.

She made a few more notes on the file. "So, I'm holding off on other tests unless the symptoms get worse. The water aerobics class is fine, in fact, any regular exercise, but just be careful if you start to feel any lightheadedness. You're still taking the prenatal vitamins?" Julie waited.

Hunt looked at Sarah.

She nodded.

"Good," Hunt said, and turned to Julie. "Anything else she should be taking?"

Sarah patted him on the thigh. "Easy, Hunt, I've got this under control." She rubbed her forehead. "I'm taking iron, too, okay?"

"Problem with constipation?" Julie asked. She looked at Sarah. Her tongue could be seen pressing her cheek out. Her eyes danced in obvious amusement.

Sarah looked at the ceiling. "I'm taking the stool softener you prescribed. Do you need the details?"

Julie wisely went back to examining her notes. "Another thing, are you going to Lamaze classes?"

"Yeah, I've done two already—with Katarina. She's my birthing partner, as you know. But I got an e-mail from her over the weekend that with school cancelled for some teachers' convention, she and Ben are taking Matt to visit colleges, and she won't be able to make it tonight. So I think I'll just give it a miss for one week."

Julie rested her chin on her hand. "Gee, Matt is already at that stage? What is he, a junior?"

"Yeah, can you believe it? Apparently, people start this college thing when their kids still have a year to go. I think Ben and Katarina are freaking out about it."

Hunt held up his hand. "Excuse me. About this Lamaze class thing. Couldn't I be your, what did you call it, birth partner, for the one class?" He pulled out his BlackBerry. "It's…ah…when?"

Julie studied him, then glanced at Sarah. "And here I thought you were the compulsively organized one among us."

Sarah ignored Julie's comment. "It's really not necessary," she said quickly to Hunt.

"Don't listen to her. I think it's a good idea," Julie said more loudly and only a beat later. She scanned her notes with a smirk. "Lastly, have you picked out a pediatrician?"

Sarah shook her head. "I know there're two groups in town, and I thought I'd ask around to get some opinions and then set up an office visit. I'm sure my trusty sidekick here will be happy to come along," she said somewhat condescendingly.

Julie laughed and closed Sarah's file. "I'll let you two work out the details. That's it for today. You can make the appointment for next week at the same time."

"That soon?" Hunt asked, getting to his feet. He slipped his phone into his pocket and readjusted his jacket under his arm.

"It's just the regular routine." Sarah got up slowly. "Come, Mother Hen. You can put that appointment on your calendar, too, if it makes you feel better."

They made the appointment with the receptionist,

and Hunt assisted Sarah with her jacket as they headed outside for the car. Slipping into their new routine, he helped her with her seat belt, which she appreciated, she really did, but somehow…

"You know, I appreciate your interest and all your help—I really do—but you don't need to worry about my every need."

"You bake cookies, I worry, okay?"

"Funny, you don't come across as a worrier. You know, you really should lower your stress levels. It's not good for you."

"I'm not working. I'm financially secure. I have a housekeeper. I have a constant supply of baked goods. My major options during the day are which route do I walk the dog, and when to turn on CNN. If I have any less stress I'll turn into a sea slug."

"I get the point. But really, you don't need to mother me. I'm actually quite good at being independent." She placed her hand on his chin and looked him in the eye.

"Do you really think I'm doing this because I want you to think of me as your mother?" He rubbed his chin back and forth against her palm.

Sarah felt herself blushing and went to lower her hand.

Hunt caught it and cupped it in his. He brought his head closer. The black centers of his gray-blue eyes were large. His expression conveyed sincerity. And more— much more.

Sarah shifted her eyes slightly downward to his open mouth. She felt his light, warm breath on her skin, his long fingers gently massaging her hand.

"I don't want you to be my mother, either," she said in a whisper.

"Sarah, watch me," he said.

She looked up.

He smiled. "Wow! I didn't even need a treat to get you to respond, but maybe this will do."

Then he kissed her, hard and swift. She took her hand from his grasp and brought her arms to his shoulders, and she kissed back with a longing that was so deep it almost hurt. It was like diving into an unknown abyss— but one that beckoned with flames of desire that licked at her heels and scorched her insides.

Finally, he drew back.

Slowly, she opened her eyes. "Wow is right. You're going to have to turn on the defroster to unfog the windows." She fanned her face.

He leaned forward and kissed her again, this time a series of nips and nibbles on her lips.

She could feel the heat rising again, and she didn't even bother with the excuse of hormones. She knew better.

It was all Hunt. She liked him. More than liked him. She hadn't come looking for it, and she'd certainly tried to avoid it. But no matter what, she couldn't kid herself any longer.

Maybe she was attracted to him because it proved that she was still a desirable woman. And maybe he was attracted to her because it proved an inner potency, a life force that had been restored.

If it was mutually self-serving, so be it. But it was also no use pretending any longer that something wasn't happening between them. And that something was inevitable, as well.

So what did she say after such a revelation?

"Gee, that was a novel way to wrap up a prenatal visit" was the best she could come up with.

"You think that wraps things up?"

"You and I both know it doesn't," she said. There was no point in being coy.

"Tell me you don't have a patient scheduled anytime soon," he said.

She looked at her watch. Nine-thirty. "Unfortunately, I've got one at ten." She sighed. The inevitable would have to be postponed. "Listen, just drop me off at work directly. It won't hurt to get to the office early."

"No way. We still have time to drive home, pick up the Hairy Demon and walk to work."

"But I thought you couldn't stand walking to work?"

Hunt absentmindedly rubbed the scratch on the side of his face, a reminder of yesterday's dog obedience class. "Maybe I'm trying to get in good with my personal trainer so she will take pity on me this evening?"

"You want pity?" Sarah smirked.

"Honey, I'll take it any way I can get it." Hunt bit back a smile. "Besides, just remember all this walking is increasing my stamina."

"Thank you for embedding that thought in my head for the whole day," she said.

"Good." Hunt started the engine. "Well, I'm glad we got that whole mothering thing worked out."

"SO DID YOU WANT ME TO PICK UP anything besides cranberry juice and baking soda at the supermarket?" Hunt asked as they approached the parking lot behind Sarah's office. He took a much needed moment to recoup his breath after the brisk walk, and Fred obligingly stopped to sniff the azaleas planted around the building.

He had to admit, though, the walk was getting easier. Progress, even in baby steps, he told himself.

"That's baking powder, not soda," Sarah corrected.

"Powder, soda. What's the big difference?"

"Pretty big if you want a chocolate cake tonight, trust me."

"I do. I do." He leaned over and snuck a kiss.

"Hey, are you trying to destroy my professional image outside my place of work?" She grabbed his sleeve and pulled him close.

"I'd like to destroy a lot more than your image, but a sense of decorum and not wanting to embarrass Fred restrains me from doing so."

She laughed, and they walked arm in arm to the door. Fred, perhaps sensing that this moment of shared happiness might result in a treat, trotted along, a model of the well-trained dog.

Hunt was starting to think there was hope for the animal after all. He was warm and furry, which were two bonuses up front. If he could only learn to do things like walk nicely on a leash, not cower every time he saw a strange man, and not eat stray loafers, he would be perfect.

Sarah turned the doorknob. "Rufus will be so impressed to see how Fred has improved in just one day. What a good boy," Sarah said in that singsongy voice that dog owners assumed when they were praising their pets. "And you know what, Fred? You'll even get

a chance to show him now. He's my first appointment."
She opened the door.

And stopped dead in her tracks.

CHAPTER TWENTY

HUNT NEARLY RAN UP HER HEELS, especially with Fred pulling him toward a set of chairs in the waiting room.

"Rufus," Hunt said, acknowledging the object of Fred's interest.

"Sarah?" The voice belonged to a man who stood by the counter across the room.

Hunt turned toward the voice—and the man. He was in his early thirties, clean shaven, and with short, gelled brown hair. He wore high-end workout clothes and the latest running shoes. He positively glowed with health, like an advertisement for a sports drink.

Hunt hated him instantly.

"Zach," Sarah said curtly before abruptly turning to Rufus. "Rufus, we can go right back, if you want?"

"Not before I give my buddy Fred here a treat. What a good dog. You're not scared of me anymore, are you?" Rufus fumbled in his pocket and produced a liver treat.

Fred gobbled it down quickly, tilted his head and waited for more.

The man she'd called "Zach" held out his hand toward her protruding baby belly. "You're…you're…" He fumbled for words. "You're *really* pregnant."

Sarah barely graced him with a glance. "So my

doctor tells me." She pressed one hand to the small of her back.

Hunt stepped forward next to Sarah. "I don't think we've met. I'm Hunt Phox. And I gather you're Zach?"

Zach nodded. "Pleased to meet you. Nice dog you've got there." Zach made the mistake of reaching out to pet Fred, who immediately scampered behind Hunt and Sarah, slinking his body low to the ground.

"He's shy, isn't he?" Zach backpedaled.

"No, he just has good taste." Sarah turned around and made kissing noises to Fred. "It's all right, Fred. Zach was just leaving."

"But, Sarah, I came by to talk to you," Zach said, a pleading note to his voice.

"Not now. I've got a client who demands my professional attention. Unless you've made an appointment and have a doctor's prescription…." She looked over at Rosemary who was pretending to be busy on the computer. "Does he have an appointment?" Sarah asked her.

Rosemary lifted her head. "Oh, ah…" She made a cursory glance at the printout of the day's clients. "Not that I see here."

Sarah held up her hands. "In which case, I will say goodbye. Goodbye." She offered the briefest of waves and shifted her attention to Rufus. "Shall we begin the torture?" she asked playfully.

"Not before I give my friend Fred another treat," Rufus said. He produced another liver bit. "Fred, watch me."

Fred watched as perfectly as if he'd been doing it his whole life.

"You've been working hard with him, Hunt. I can tell."

"Actually, it's been a joint effort, so you should compliment Sarah, too," Hunt said.

"You own a dog now?" Zach asked.

Sarah rubbed her forehead. "It's a long story." She moved to go down the hallway.

"Sarah?" Hunt held out his hand to stop her.

She looked over her shoulder, her eyebrows raised.

"Maybe you should just take a moment to hear what he has to say?"

Sarah shook her head. "I'm sorry, Hunt, but you don't have the right to tell me how to treat my ex-fiancé."

"You're right." He paused. "When should I pick you up?"

She narrowed her eyes. "Let's see. I've got to go to the hospital in the afternoon, but I can just walk over during my lunch break. It's not far. I have to see a bunch of patients there, but I tell you what. Why don't you check with Rosemary about my schedule? It's on her computer, and then you can just meet me at the hospital reception desk when it's time."

"I've got a better idea. How about we meet at Dunkin' Donuts across the street to get a bite to eat at lunch, and then I can drive you over to the hospital? I was planning on checking out the health club in the shopping center anyway, and that way I'll have company for lunch. I usually have to eat alone, you know."

Sarah grinned. "Are you trying to make me feel sorry for you?"

"But you'll meet me, won't you?" he pressed.

"Okay, okay, but be there at noon. If you're even two

minutes late, I'm leaving. No excuses." She swiped the air with her hand.

"No problem. Noon on the dot. I'll even make sure to reserve a table in a cozy, private corner."

Sarah sought out Rosemary. "Can you believe this guy?"

Rosemary rested her chin on her hands. "I think it's sweet. I wish someone would offer to meet me at Dunkin' Donuts."

"Rosemary! You're married with two grown sons!"

"Exactly! Be in my position and you'd understand."

"That gives me an idea," Rufus said. "I might just take Thelma later this afternoon. I saw a flyer in the mail with a coupon for their seasonal pumpkin donuts. She'll be tickled pink."

"Okay, okay, I get the message. Anyone who's anyone is going to be at Dunkin' Donuts. But like I said—noon." Sarah didn't bother to look back as she trotted down the hallway. Rufus had to hustle to catch up.

"I'll say goodbye now, too, Rosemary." Zach raised his hand. He nodded at Hunt, crossed the room and opened the door to leave.

Hunt saluted Rosemary. "So, I'll call you later this afternoon to get the boss's schedule." Then he sprinted after Zach. "Hey, Zach, hold up," he called, pulling Fred with him.

As soon as he was through the door, the dog spotted a squirrel digging in the stones. He lunged toward it, almost dislocating Hunt's shoulder. The squirrel, showing a keen sense of survival, scurried up a drainpipe attached to the low office building. Fred began leaping as far as the leash would allow him in a futile attempt to reach the squirrel, now tantalizingly out of reach atop the gutter. Fred watched the twitching tail and sprung upward over and over despite Hunt's commands.

"Some dog you got there. He should be in a circus," Zach said.

Hunt gave him an exasperated smile. "Let me tell you about this dog."

KATARINA SPOKE ANIMATEDLY into her phone. "We've just gotten out of this information lecture given by the admissions people at Yale, and now we're waiting to be divided up into groups for a tour."

"Who's that?" Ben mouthed.

Katarina covered the phone and whispered, *"Babička."* They were milling on the lawn among a large group of high school students and their parents. The admissions offices were located on the elegant tree-lined Hillhouse Avenue in New Haven. Originally the mansions on the street had been private abodes. Now they served as administration buildings or departmental offices.

She nodded as she listened to Lena speak. "Yeah, I agree. Yale is very impressive from what little we've seen of it." She listened some more. "Yes, the weather's great. In fact, we saw online that the leaves are already beginning to change in Massachusetts and Vermont, so we're thinking of extending the trip from three to four days. Maybe go up to the Berkshires besides going on to Boston?" She looked at Ben for confirmation.

"I want to get the full maple syrup experience," he said, coming over. He hugged her around the waist and kissed her lightly on the side of her hair.

She smiled, momentarily distracted. "What? Could

you repeat that? You're fading in and out." She slapped Ben away when he started to ruffle her hair.

"Okay, I hear you now. No, *Babička,* I haven't spoken to Sarah recently. I mean, I emailed her on Sunday when we decided to take this trip." She paused to listen. "No, I don't really know what she plans to do about child care. I know she's got some maternity leave coming, and I think she spoke with Amanda about maybe working part-time."

The guides for the tour began calling for people to gather around them.

"Listen, *Babička,* I really have to go… What? Fine, but I'll pass you to Matt, but, you know, you were the one who called me and was doing all the talking. Oh, never mind…" She tapped Matt on the back. The teen-ager was talking to another boy who'd sat next to him during the information session. "It's *Babička.* She wants to talk to—and I quote—'my favorite person.'" She handed off the phone, and Matt sidled away to talk.

Ben looked down at Katarina. "What was that all about? Everything all right?"

Katarina shrugged her shoulders. "She seems fine. She just wanted to chat—about the trip, then about Sarah. Nothing special."

Matt returned and handed back the phone. "Let's join that group," he said, pointing to the one where his newly found friend had gravitated. "Only could you both not stand right next to me? This is my tour, after all."

Ben made a face to Katarina.

Katarina waved it off. "No problem, Matt. By the way, did *Babička* say anything special?"

Matt thumbed through a large blue information folder and tried to act casual. "Nothing. She just wanted to know if I knew how to play the 'Wedding March.' Then she told me that Yale has this collection of rare musical instruments that sounds really cool. You think we have time to visit it after the tour?" He looked at Ben and Katarina.

"Cool," Ben said, then looked at Katarina. "Cool?" he asked her.

Katarina was buried in thought for a moment, and it took a beat before she responded. "Yeah, fine. Cool. Whatever. Just let me make one more call."

CHAPTER TWENTY-ONE

SARAH'S PLEASURE AT DISCOVERING Hunt holding open the door for her at Dunkin' Donuts disappeared as soon as she entered the fast-food establishment. "Oh, no. This wasn't part of the deal."

"I asked him to come," Hunt said.

"Well, you can un-ask him." She crossed her arms in front of her.

Zach pushed his chair back from a corner table and walked over to join them. He seemed at a loss as to where to put his hands and ended up clasping them behind his back. Prince Charles he wasn't.

Hunt touched Sarah's sleeve. "I really think you should talk to him."

"It would just take a minute. I promise," Zach said.

"C'mon, Sarah. What can be the harm? A few minutes? Besides, I spoke with him this morning, and I think he just wants to do the right thing."

She shook her head at Hunt. "It's just not that easy. Or that simple. And he is no longer part of my life." Then she paused. She refused to lose it in a public place.

She forced herself to look at Zach. "I don't know what Hunt said or implied to you, but my bottom line is, forget it. You signed away any legal rights to the baby. And I don't need you or want you involved. End of story."

She started to leave, but Hunt gripped her arm.

"Sarah, just give the guy five minutes. If you won't talk to him for yourself, talk to him for the sake of the baby. I never really knew my father, never was given the opportunity to get to know him. And look how that screwed me up. I know how important this can be. If you don't do this, you'll regret it. Trust me." He held her arm and stared at her squarely. "If you talk to him this once, I promise never to bug you about this ever again, okay?"

Sarah scratched her temple. Finally she looked up. "Okay. You make a convincing argument, especially the part about how screwed up you are. But I swear. Five minutes, and that's it."

Hunt did his best not to look too pleased with himself and ushered her to the table in the corner by the window. It faced the interior courtyard of the old-fashioned shopping center, anchored at one end by an upscale supermarket and the other by a Rite Aid drugstore. In between were local shops and restaurants catering to everyday needs from screwdrivers to birthday cards.

He pulled out a chair for her next to Zach. Then he sat on her other side. "Can I get you both something? Coffee? A donut?"

Zach shook his head. "I never have fried foods or take caffeine."

Sarah rolled her eyes. "Such a purist." She leveled a gaze at Hunt. "You can get me a bagel with cream cheese. And why don't you get yourself a glazed donut? They have extra calories."

"Always looking out for my welfare." Hunt slipped off his jacket and joined the lunchtime line at the front of the store.

Sarah watched him go then turned to look out the

window. She saw two young mothers with strollers. A toddler ran on ahead, pushing a doll in a ministroller of its own. It all appeared so happy, so innocent. *Will my life ever be so uncomplicated?* Sarah wondered.

"He seems like a nice guy," Zach interrupted her thoughts. "He told me how you're staying with him until the baby comes, maybe even a while beyond that, which I thought was pretty generous."

Sarah reluctantly dragged her gaze back to the man sitting so near. She studied him. Zach looked unchanged. No, that wasn't true. He was still handsome and fit, but he no longer conveyed that serenity, the comfortable sense of purpose that she had once found so attractive. Or had that serenity merely been an illusion?

She pursed her lips. "I said I would sit here for five minutes. If you want to use that time to discuss my rooming situation, fine by me."

Zach straightened the napkin container in the middle of the table. "I know this is hard for you, and I appreciate you're willing to listen to me." He looked up from fussing and drew a large breath. "I want to apologize."

Sarah pressed the tip of her tongue on the edge of her top teeth. "And now, having said that, you expect me to accept your apology?"

Zach shook his head. "No, not really. I mean, sure, it would make me feel a lot better, but I'm not expecting you to forgive me—not after what I did."

"You lied to me." Sarah's expression was bleak.

"I lied to you. I lied to myself—for most of my life, in fact." Zach swallowed. "And when I finally accepted who I was, I was too frightened to just come out and let you know. Sneaking around behind your back was cowardly."

"It wasn't exactly behind my back on our wedding day."

"I know. I know. That was really stupid. I wasn't thinking. The whole wedding thing just spiraled out of control. I didn't know what to do."

"You wanted to be caught, didn't you?" Sarah asked quietly. She peered at him intently.

Zach sighed. "I guess. I guess I wanted you to be the one to call the whole thing off instead of me taking responsibility."

"Well, we all have moments where we've reneged on our responsibilities," Sarah admitted. She could feel herself softening. But it was one thing to understand, another to forgive. Even now, months afterward, the humiliation hurt. Oh, the shock may have worn off, but she still felt the anger. "You devastated me that day, you know."

"I know what I did was cruel and unforgivable—" Zach started to speak but held up his hand as if to give himself more time to choose his words carefully. "Okay, please, don't take this in the wrong way, because I mean it as a compliment. What I want to say is I don't really think you were devastated."

Sarah laughed sardonically.

Zach held up his hand again. "Hear me out. You know, I always admired you because you seemed so independent and sure of yourself. I kind of felt like our relationship—and by extension, our marriage— was some kind of an add-on to your life, not a central part."

"But you knew how much I wanted a family," Sarah protested.

Zach leaned forward. "But did you want me as a

husband and life partner, or was I just one piece of your plan for a family?"

Sarah covered her mouth and chin with her hands. She breathed in slowly. "I don't know. Right now I'm so mixed up. I can't even remember." She noticed the faint lines around his mouth and the enlarged pores along the creases of his nose, all the imperfections that she had never really seen before. "It's funny that you thought of me as so self-assured, because I've never felt that way. I always thought that you were the one who was so together. Did I ever really know you? Did you ever really know me?"

"Did we really know ourselves?" Zach asked.

"Here's the food and drink," Hunt announced. He had a large coffee in one hand and two bags in the other.

Sarah reached across the back of her chair for her backpack and stood up. "I don't think I have time for it now. I need to get going to the hospital. You can drive me, and I'll pick up something later."

"But your bagel?" Hunt waggled the bag.

"Keep it." She heard Zach push his chair back, the legs scraping against the floor.

"Sarah? About the baby. I know I signed away any rights, so there's no need to worry," he said, as if sensing the tightness in her shoulders. "I'm not here to contest that. I just wanted to say, that if you need anything, any help, I'm here. I may have been a coward when it came to admitting what I am, but I'm not one to run away from responsibility now. Okay?"

Sarah swallowed. "I'll keep that in mind. But…but… it's complicated."

Zach nodded. "I understand."

She nodded goodbye and left, forcing Hunt to play catch-up.

He juggled the coffee and the bags, and when some coffee spilled through the hole in the travel lid, he licked it off his fingers. "Slow down a minute," he pleaded. He rested his paper cup on the car roof and fished the keys out of his pocket. "So, what did he say?"

As the locks clicked, Sarah opened the door and got in, shutting the door in Hunt's face. When he circled the car and got in, she refused to look across the console. "Just drive," she said. "Just drive."

SARAH PUSHED THROUGH the revolving door to the hospital entrance, smiling at the two volunteers manning the reception desk. They were the same two chatty women who had been manning the desk on Mondays the whole time Sarah had lived in Grantham. Their ruthless permanents hadn't altered in the seven years.

She tucked her chin into the collar of her barn coat and took a left turn, trudging past the cafeteria without bothering to stop. She headed quickly toward the staff locker rooms. But before she changed into the regulation top and donned her I.D. badge she made a beeline for the bathroom.

She desperately had to pee. Not that that was anything new. More than that, she desperately needed privacy. She found an empty bathroom stall, walked in and flipped the lever to lock the door. She bit down on her bottom lip and closed her eyes.

And let the tears come.

She cried silently and deeply, recounting all the screwups of her life, all her emotional bumps and bruises, and all the ways she had hurt others and had been hurt herself. When at last the tears stopped coming, she wiped her nose with the back of her hand and then reached into the zipped section of her knapsack for her cell phone.

She went to Favorites and hit the number that usually was a chore to call. She waited, listening to the dial tone. Finally, the familiar voice picked up and answered.

"Mom? It's Sarah," she said, the tears starting anew. "Mommy?" Her voice went up. "I need to talk to you."

CHAPTER TWENTY-TWO

SARAH TAPPED OUT the security code and entered Hunt's house. She had left word that Julie was going to drive her home from the hospital, so there had been no need for him to come pick her up. For once, she was grateful for the indulgence of taking an elevator upstairs. She got out at the living room, and Fred bounded toward her, doing his tail-wagging dance in honor of her return. She smiled—who wouldn't?—and bent to rub his ears. Fred snuggled against her leg before performing a pirouette toward the bag of treats on the counter. Dutifully, Sarah walked over and reached in the bag.

"Fred, watch me," she commanded, well trained after only two days. Fred responded, and Sarah gave him his treat. Then he rushed away to reclaim a tennis ball from under the coffee table.

She heard footsteps coming down the stairway. Sarah knew it was Hunt. He wore socks but no shoes. There was a red crease line running down his cheek, and he hadn't bothered to put on his glasses. He looked as though he'd just woken up from a nap. She also saw that he was carrying a medicine bottle in his hand.

"Everything all right?" she asked, not wanting to show her concern but doing so anyway.

"Just a headache." He headed toward the overhead kitchen cabinets and removed a glass. He filled it in the sink and popped a few tablets. "I tested my culinary skills and made us chili for dinner," he said. "I can't guarantee the results, but at least we won't go hungry before your Lamaze class tonight."

She registered for the first time the smell of slightly burned food simmering on the stove. She hadn't counted on him ministering to her needs, even if inexpertly. His kindness almost had her burst into tears yet again. She had been a faucet all afternoon.

No, what she had expected was for him to chide her about not needing his driving services, followed by an intense questioning about her conversation with Zach. Was he being polite, giving her distance, or merely putting her on the spot, forcing her to make the first move? She was too tired, physically and emotionally to know.

She shook her head. "Listen, that's…ah…nice of you—"

"'Nice.' Ouch," Hunt said without his lilt.

She shook her head. "It's nothing personal." It was totally personal. "I'm just kind of pooped right now. Do you mind if I take a nap before we have to go out?" She glanced at her watch. "We've got about an hour."

"Sure, no problem. Should I wake you?"

"No, I'll set the alarm on my phone." She started for the stairs, and Fred got up and trotted along with her, rushing to go up first. He bounded up and waited for her at the top of the stairs, his tail wagging as usual.

That was the great thing about dogs, she realized. The world could be falling apart, but they were always eager to join in. She rested her hand on the railing and was about to begin what seemed like a very long climb when she stopped. "Hunt?" she called out.

He had wandered over to the couch and picked up a section of the newspaper. He looked up in response to her voice.

"I thought you should know. I decided to let Zach into the baby's life even though he has no legal rights. I called him and told him this afternoon. I'm still not sure it's the right thing, but I'm willing to do it—for the baby. So, you won."

He dropped the paper on the coffee table. "It was never a question of winning."

"Okay, whatever. I just—just—wanted to say that you were right, but that still doesn't mean I don't resent the way you handled the situation."

"You would have talked to Zach any other way?"

She worked her lower lip. "Probably not, but I still don't appreciate being manipulated." She put a foot on the first riser, but halted. "I called my mother. She agrees with you, if it makes you feel any better."

"The real question is, do you?"

"I'M SO GLAD TO SEE YOU all here again tonight," the Lamaze instructor said in a cheery, energetic voice. "Sarah, I see you brought a new partner."

Sarah hugged her pillow. "This is Hunt. He's helping me out while Katarina is away this week." She pulled him down next to her on the carpeted floor.

"Hunt. Nice to see you. I'm Eliza, and we're delighted you've come."

Hunt looked around stealthily. Some of the couples he recognized from the water aerobics class. He wasn't sure since they had their clothes on. He leaned toward Sarah. "Was I supposed to bring a pillow, too?" She had been less than communicative the whole way over, mumbling only a few clipped responses.

"Only the moms-to-be bring pillows like the ones they plan to bring to the hospital," she said, and shushed him as Eliza launched into her spiel.

"Tonight, we'll practice our breathing techniques and relaxation exercises some more, but first I thought I'd play this short DVD. It shows actual pictures of women and their partners during labor and giving birth. It includes both vaginal and Caesarean births and discusses possible complications—not that we want that or anticipate any problems, but so that we can be prepared in case they may occur. Before I start it, though, I thought I'd do show-and-tell."

She reached into a totebag on the chair behind the desk. "Not many doctors perform deliveries with forceps anymore, but let me show you what they look like." She held up what looked like giant salad tongs.

Hunt rested his head in his hand.

"Squeamish?" Sarah asked under her breath.

He shook his head. The headache was getting worse despite the Tylenol. It was a constant piercing pain in the back of his head.

"I assume all of you have been doing your Kegel exercises to develop your pelvic floor muscles to help prevent tears and possible episiotomies." Eliza mimicked the contractions with her fingers. "But in case you and your physician decide an episiotomy is necessary, I thought I'd show you what the knife looks like."

Hunt rubbed his ear and moaned softly.

Sarah laughed under her breath. "My hero. Wait till you see the Caesarean!"

"Katarina owes me."

THE NEXT MORNING Hunt dragged himself out of bed only after Fred sat on him and began licking his hands. He'd had a fitful night's sleep at best, getting up repeatedly to take more Tylenol but to no effect. The ache in his head, if anything, was worse than ever.

"Okay, buddy," he said, swinging his legs to the side. A surge of pain almost caused him to black out. He blinked and breathed in slowly. Maybe with some coffee, he'd feel more human.

He glanced at the clock and swore. Nine o'clock. Sarah must be having fits because she was sure to be late to the office, even *if* he drove her. He stood up, wobbly on his feet. It was going to be interesting driving if this headache didn't let up. Fred danced around his feet, and he tried to concentrate on not tripping over the silly mutt.

Barefoot, wearing sweatpants and an old Grantham University T-shirt, he padded down the stairs, ready to fend off her wrath. Only to find silence.

And a tin of chocolate chip cookies. Another of lemon squares. And an apple pie covered in plastic wrap.

A note was propped up against the pie.

Hunt—I decided to walk to work on my own. I just need a little more space to myself. Eat as much as you want. I certainly don't need the calories. S. P.S. I've already fed and walked Fred. Don't let the little monster try to trick you into more food.

Hunt surveyed the baked goods. She must have been up half the night. The lemon bars would normally be the most tempting, but the thought of moving his jaw...

Fred barked.

Hunt felt his cheek. It was warm. No, more than warm. Hot. He moved his hand around. His jaw was tender to the touch. So was his ear. It was swollen and felt like it was on fire. He moved his fingers downward. The lymph node below his ear was enlarged.

Fred barked more loudly.

Hunt ignored it and headed for the powder room down the hall. The dog followed, nipping at the baggy material of Hunt's sweatpants.

"Quit it, Fred," Hunt yelled. He never yelled. But then he'd never felt like this before. He pushed open the bathroom door and went to the mirrored medicine cabinet over the sink. He leaned in close. The whole left side of his face was swollen to the size of a melon. His ear was grotesquely stretched out of shape and an angry red.

His first thought was cancer. That it had come back.

He gripped the edge of the sink. The pain was becoming blinding.

"Breathe out, slowly," he told himself out loud. "See, Lamaze class can come in handy after all," he said, but the joke fell flat. He continued to think out loud. "More than likely, it's…ah…some kind of reaction to a bug bite or something like that." He exhaled. "There's no reason to think it's cancer when I was perfectly clean at my last checkup only a few weeks ago."

He turned, still holding the sink, and found Fred lying down, his face between his paws, looking at him with a worried expression. "It's okay, Fred buddy. I'm going to take care of the situation. Don't worry." He pressed his hand at the back of his head where the pain was centered.

My phone. Where the hell is my phone? He closed his eyes and concentrated. That's right, he had left it on the coffee table last night after coming in from class.

He staggered into the living room, grabbed the phone and flopped on the couch. Fred jumped up next to him, and for once, Hunt didn't shoo him off. Instead, he let the dog curl up next to him and rubbed his warm fur as he worked his phone to find his contact list. He dialed the obvious choice.

After only one ring, Ben answered. "What's up, bro?"

"I was wondering if you could do me a favor?" Hunt closed his eyes and rocked methodically back and forth.

"What kind of favor? We're at this B and B in Lenox, Massachusetts, and unless you want some of these fancy curtains they sell in the gift shop, I'm not much good to you."

"That's right. I forgot. You're making the grand college tour." Hunt tried to concentrate. "Listen, you wouldn't happen to have Katarina's grandmother's phone number, would you?"

"Interested in getting some free homemade cakes, are you?"

Ben thought of the mounds of carbohydrates and butter sitting on the counter. "No, dessert is not something I lack at the moment. Just a small favor from someone nearby."

"Okay, wait a minute. I'll just ask Katarina. She's on her phone."

Hunt waited.

"Hunt, you still there?" Ben asked. "Here's Lena's

home number, but Katarina says she might already be out playing tennis. Did you want her cell, too?"

"Just give me the home number. I wouldn't want to interrupt her game. Meanwhile, enjoy the potpourri for me." Hunt hung up quickly and dialed Lena's number.

The answering machine picked up after six rings, and Hunt heard Lena's lyrical Eastern European accent on the recorded message.

Hunt waited for the beep. "Mrs. Zemanova, Lena—" Hunt wet his lips, trying to decide how best to put this without raising any alarms. He certainly didn't want the world descending on him, worrying about something that was probably no big deal.

"Lena, it's Hunt Phox," he continued. "I have to be somewhere unexpectedly this morning, and I was wondering if you could do me a favor—come walk my dog, Fred, at noon? His leash is in the foyer, on the side table by the door, and there's a bag of treats in the drawer. He'll come if you just hold one out to him. The code for the front door is as follows." He rattled off the numbers.

"If for some reason you can't make it, don't worry. I'll try Rufus next. He already knows Fred. If I'm held up any later than this morning, though, I may give you another call about feeding him. Thanks."

Hunt hung up and scrolled through his contact list for Rufus.

Rufus picked up right away, and Hunt explained his predicament.

"No problem, Hunt. I was about to leave for my physio appointment with Sarah, as a matter of fact. I'm running late as it is, but this way I can just use you as an excuse."

"Sorry, I didn't mean to hold you up any further.

Forget about coming over. I'll just give someone else a call. And no need to mention anything to her. She's got enough on her plate as it is. Thanks." Hunt rang off and let his hand fall to his lap. So much for asking Rufus to drive him to the emergency room. He was running out of ideas.

That left his mother, but if past experience were any guide, she didn't deal well with hospitals when it came to actual sickness. He unconsciously patted and stroked the dog.

And then it came to him. Hunt lifted his arm and scanned the contact list again, searching for the latest entry. When he reached it, he pressed the name and heard a response.

Hunt swallowed. "Zach. I need a favor."

CHAPTER TWENTY-THREE

"So how's the trip? Are you ready to abandon your consulting business and New Jersey for the Berkshires and making goat cheese and knitting socks, or whatever people do up in New England?" Sarah asked Katarina.

Sarah adjusted the phone at her ear and leaned back in her office chair, glancing at her watch. It was a little after nine o'clock, and Rufus was running late. She'd make sure to give him grief.

Earlier, she'd walked to work by herself. She hadn't bothered to knock on Hunt's bedroom door when she went down to the kitchen. Just as well, since she didn't feel like justifying her behavior. She knew he would tell her it was foolish. But Sarah had needed to get out on her own, clear her mind, recharge her soul.

She wanted to hate Hunt for forcing her to confront her demons, but in the light of a new day, and in the solitude of a brisk walk on a fall morning, she couldn't. Because it turned out that her demons really weren't so demonic.

What she had needed to face was her own expectations, her own insecurities, and her own sense of self-worth. In the end, she had gone running to Mommy. No, that wasn't true. She had called for sympathy and for unqualified love. But she had also called for reassurance from one individual to another that even though life was sometimes messy, it would get better.

At least until the next bout of messiness.

So where did Hunt fit into all this? Was he the problem or was he the answer?

"Remind me never to book a B and B again," Katarina went on, oblivious to the big thoughts bumping around in Sarah's brain. "Ben's just too big. Whichever way he turns there's some knickknack waiting for him to run into, and I can't tell you how many times he's hit his head on the crossbeams."

Sarah heard a ringing in the background and what sounded like Ben answering another phone.

"And all the froufrou—it's definitely upping his level of surliness," Katarina continued. "Wait a minute. Ben's trying to get my attention."

Sarah fiddled with her cup of herbal tea and wished she had packed some of the chocolate cookies she'd baked during the night.

"Sorry about that." Katarina was back. "That's Hunt calling Ben on his cell. He asked for *Babička*'s phone number. Do you have any idea why he'd want it?"

"Not really. We've had a little excitement, Hunt and I, but nothing to bother her with."

"The baby? Are you all right?"

"Fine. We're all fine." Sarah waved her hand. "It's slightly complicated. I'll tell you about it when you get back. In the meantime, enjoy yourself. Don't think about any of us."

"I'll try not to, though it's hard with everyone calling all the time."

"I don't call *all* the time!" Sarah protested.

"No, I don't mean you. I guess I was speaking of

my grandmother. Listen, you've got to hear the latest bombshell. She called me last night wanting to know what I thought about Wanda moving in with her."

"Wanda? Move in with your grandmother? I know they're good friends, but…"

"She tells me it would be her personal version of an assisted-living facility. The two of them would pool their money and help each other out. That way, even on fixed incomes, they'd both have more flexibility. Naturally, I said Ben and I would be glad to help out if it was just a question of money, but she rejected that immediately. To make a long story short, I promised to get together with the two of them when I get back and run the numbers."

Sarah heard some loud swearing in the background.

"Oops! I got to go," Katarina said quickly. "Ben just managed to get a shirt button caught on a curtain tieback."

JULIE STRODE THROUGH the Emergency Room. She turned her head from side to side, acknowledging the nurses at the station, the huddle of medical students trailing the E.R. docs, and the patients filling the rooms and hallway gurneys. Business was certainly brisk, especially for a Tuesday.

She was the obstetrician on call from noon to midnight, and since there were no immediate emergencies, her first stop was the cafeteria followed by sleep. She'd been up the night before with a protracted delivery, and after seeing several patients early in the morning, she was ready for some shut-eye.

With a purposeful, long gait, she traversed the E.R.

and was close to the double doors that led to the rest of the hospital when a well-worn Docksider boat shoe caught her attention—plus the fact that it was attached to a long, male leg in loose sweatpants. The man's face was hidden behind a pillow so she couldn't tell who it was. But the pillow was definitely familiar. It was one Julie had needlepointed and given to Sarah.

"Hunt? Hunt Phox?" She stopped next to the gurney he was lying on in the hallway. When the E.R. was over-flowing, they put patients wherever there was space.

She placed a hand gently on his knee. "Hunt? Is that you?"

Hunt slowly removed the pillow, and Julie immediately saw the extreme redness and swelling. She also recognized the obvious pain. She leaned closer. "What's going on?" she asked in a well-schooled, calm voice.

Hunt swallowed. "It seems I've got an infection. I thought I had a reaction to a bug bite on my face, but they found a scratch on my ear, probably one of the dogs in the obedience class got me by accident. Anyway, it looks like it's gotten infected—cellu—cellu—something." He closed the eye on the side of his head that was grossly distorted.

"Cellulitis," Julie clarified. "You told them about the Hodgkin's and that your immune system is suppressed after chemo, right?"

"Yeah, first thing. That seemed to get their attention." Hunt shifted to face her. "I'm supposed to be getting some morphine for the pain, and I think they're going to start an antibiotic drip. A nurse already put in a line." He raised his arm to show her. "One of the doctor's mentioned something about a CATscan of my head and neck—just to be on the safe side."

"Who's seen you? The E.R. doctor?"

"Yeah, a resident. An ear, nose and throat person is supposed to be coming to look me over, too." Hunt winced with pain.

"Did you call your oncologist?" she asked.

"I will when I find out what's going on. Besides, he's in New York," he said. Hunt brought the pillow up next to his head again and pressed it against his ear. "Until they get me the morphine, this helps. Let me tell you. I've become a big fan of your needlepoint."

"How long have you been waiting?"

"I got here about nine-thirty."

She glanced up at the wall clock. It was almost eleven forty-five. "What the hell!"

Hunt waved his hand. "It seems there was a car wreck involving a van of nuns and a semi. That's not a bad joke, but the actual truth. Apparently, I'm way down on the list."

"Not on my list." Julie marched off to the nurses' desk.

Less than a minute later a young nurse came over and injected the morphine and hooked up an IV bottle.

Julie thanked her. She turned to Hunt. "How you feeling now? Any more pain?"

"Pain? What pain? Wow! This stuff is great! A sudden rush to the extremities, then total La La Land."

Julie patted him on the arm. "We aim to please. When did the symptoms start, anyway?"

He gave her a brief rundown of the headaches, the swelling and redness, and the excruciating pain.

She nodded. "Listen, I've got some other things to do, but I promise to check in on you later. Who's your doctor in New York, anyway? I don't think I ever got the name."

He fumbled for his cell phone in the side pocket of his sweats. "His name's Marvin Zimmerli. Unfortunately, I can't wear my glasses with all this swelling, so maybe you can find it in the Contact list."

"Sure, no problem." She deftly scrolled through his phone, and entered it into her own. She handed it back. "Get some sleep, lover boy, while you can before they start poking and prodding you some more. Let me tell you—the med students are going to lo-o-ove your case."

"Lucky me," he said.

"Lucky you." She gave him a wink.

She hit the button to swing open the double doors. As soon as they swished shut, she was on the phone to his oncologist.

BY THE TIME SARAH LET herself into Hunt's house it had been more than a full day. Instead of calling him for a lift, she had walked with her last patient who was going to the Chinese restaurant on Main Street. From there it was only two blocks.

She savored the fresh air. Hunt was probably thinking she was still sulking when she hadn't called at the end of the day. Well, she *had* texted. She couldn't help it if he hadn't bothered to reply.

She pushed open the door and immediately heard the sound of Fred's nails clipping down the stairway to the ground floor foyer. He did his customary waggles and nervous bounds, landing his front paws gently on her in a doggy hug.

"Down, Fred," she said but continued to rub his ears

and neck. Finally, she pushed him off, gave him a treat, and forced herself to trudge up the stairs instead of using the elevator.

"Hunt," she called out when she reached the living room. She didn't get any response. She went up the next flight of stairs, expecting to find him in the study or maybe lying down in his bedroom. But the place was empty.

Empty and quiet. Except for Fred following her every step of the way. He sniffed at Hunt's desk before trotting down the hallway and making a flying leap onto his unmade bed.

She walked in the room and was surprised the blinds were still drawn.

Fred stood alert in the middle of the bunched-up duvet and looked purposefully at Sarah. When she didn't react immediately, he sprang around and grabbed the corner of one of the pillows. He shook it back and forth, then flicked it with his head. It landed across the room.

Sarah walked over and picked it up, intending to put it back on the bed. But she found herself hugging it to her chest. The smell from the pillow slip wafted to her nose. It reminded her of him. Citrusy. Clean, but male.

She sat on the side of the bed, the pillow still in her arms. Then she flopped back, sinking onto the covers. Fred came over and sniffed her face. When she didn't react, he turned a few exploratory circles and collapsed next to her, Hunt's pillow squished between them.

"So where's your lord and master, Fred?" She stroked his belly.

Fred rolled over on his back, shamelessly exposing himself.

"I suppose he left a note on the kitchen counter. We'll

have to go check, I suppose, but in a minute." It felt absolutely heavenly to get off her feet and let her muscles relax and her vertebrae stretch out. She closed her eyes. "I could stay like this forever except I know that I'll have to pee any minute."

She continued to scratch the dog's stomach. There was something highly satisfying about scratching a dog, she realized. Then she shifted her head sideways to check the clock on the bedside table and noticed a pile of books. They had bar codes from the library, and they were about pregnancy and childbirth. She felt a sudden tightness in the back of her throat. Tears threatened.

Her phone sounded and she wiped her eyes and fished it out of her warm-up jacket. It was Julie.

"Hey, Julie, what's up?"

"So you haven't heard? He hasn't called you?"

"What haven't I heard, and who hasn't called me?"

"Hunt."

Sarah planted her elbow on the bed and levered herself up. "Hunt? What about Hunt?"

"He's in the hospital."

The baby kicked. Sarah tensed. She tossed aside the pillow and grabbed her abdomen. "What's wrong? The lymphoma hasn't come back, has it?"

"No, it looks like a scratch or something on his ear got infected and he's got a skin infection—cellulitis."

"How did that happen?"

"Probably because of his weakened immune system. By the time he got to the E.R. this morning, it had already traveled from his ear to the side of his face and his parotid gland and lymph nodes. Luckily, he got treatment before it had time to reach his brain and cause meningitis. These infections are nasty. They come on fast and are very dangerous. I've been in touch with his oncologist in New York—"

"Is he coming down?" Sarah sat rigid on the side of the bed. Fred had flipped over and wiggled on his belly. He pressed his nose in her hand.

"No, he didn't think he needs to. He's been in contact with the E.R. doc, the ENT specialist, and an infectious disease person they brought in from New Brunswick. He also contacted one of the local oncologists who was a former student of his. They've all been faxing and emailing him the blood work and the CT scan results."

"What about taking him in an ambulance to New York?"

"Hunt's getting very good care, and it's probably better not to move him. Listen, Sarah, this is a bad news/good news scenario. Yes, this was potentially life threatening, but the good news is that Hunt promptly got to the hospital. They're pumping him full of megaweight antibiotics, which seems to be handling the infection. He's still on morphine, but I think tonight or tomorrow they'll probably switch him to something less powerful."

"Morphine! The pain is that bad!"

"It's under control. Just like you need to be. Listen, they're going to have to keep him—"

Sarah heard a beep on her phone. "Hold on, Julie, I've got another call coming in. Maybe it's Hunt?" She switched to the other line.

"Sarah, it's Katarina. What's going on with Hunt? First he called Ben. Then I find out from *Babička* that Rufus called her to say that he'd walked the dog, that Hunt hadn't wanted him to bother you."

"Hunt's in the hospital. It looks like he's going to be okay," Sarah said, trying to stay calm despite her racing heart. "Listen, I've got Julie on the other line, and she's the one who just told me. Hunt never called to let me know. Can you believe it?"

"He probably didn't want to worry you. Anyway, *Babička* told me to tell you that she and Wanda are at some tennis tournament in Cherry Hill, but they'll be back in an hour or so. Wanda offered to come over and take care of the dog as soon as they get in."

"Okay, that's good to know. Right now I just want to get over to the hospital, even if it means driving myself."

"I wish I could help out, but we're still up in New England. Can't you wait until *Babička* gets home?"

"No, I want to go as soon as possible. He's all by himself."

"And you're the one who has to be with him now?"

Sarah didn't have time for explanations. "I'll have to talk to you later," she said, ending the conversation abruptly.

She switched to the other line. "Sorry, Julie. That was Katarina. She'd heard from her grandmother that something was wrong, but she didn't know what. Apparently, Hunt had called Rufus, too. Whatever. Where is Hunt now?"

"Last I saw him, he was still in the E.R. while they were waiting for a bed to open up upstairs."

"Wherever he is then, I'll find him." Sarah stood up. "I can't thank you enough for calling me."

"Yeah, I kind of figured you'd want to know."

"You're right, you're right. Let's leave it at that." There was nothing like a crisis to clear one's thinking. "Listen, as soon as I get some of Hunt's stuff together,

I'm going to head over to the hospital," she went on. "I suppose I could always call a taxi."

There was a pause on the other end of the line. "I've got another idea," Julie said. "But I'm not sure you're going to like it…."

SARAH PEEKED AROUND the curtain in the double room. "So, you decided you needed a little attention?" she said.

Hunt turned his head toward the sound of her voice. "Hey, you. I'm sorry I didn't call. I didn't want to bother you, especially after yesterday."

Sarah put down the grocery bag she was carrying and sat on the edge of the bed. "That was yesterday." She studied Hunt's swollen face and couldn't help wincing. "That looks like it smarts."

Hunt touched it gingerly. "Actually, it's a lot better than it was a few hours ago. The antibiotics are truly a miracle."

"And the pain?"

"Really, okay. The morphine was amazing, but I'm already onto something else. Pretty soon I'm sure I can switch to Advil. Right now they're just giving me fluids, and I get the second course of antibiotics in about an hour."

She looked across the bed at the bag hanging from the metal stand. A portable computer screen flashed the rate of flow. Satisfied, she took his hand. "Julie called and told me you were pretty bad when she first saw you in the E.R."

"It was kind of interesting, but no matter what, I will never bad-mouth her again. She waltzed in, and all of a sudden, things started happening."

"When Julie told me you were in the hospital, I immediately thought…"

"Yeah, me, too," he admitted. "But it turns out to be nothing so dramatic. More like a scratch—thank you, Toulouse—and then some kind of staph infection. So I'll just have to hold off on any dramatic deathbed scenes." He put the back of his hand to his forehead, a true diva.

Sarah shook her head. "Don't even joke about things like that! I want to punch you, but it looks like that could finish you off." She gazed out the window by his bed. It offered a view of the medical arts building across the parking lot, the tops of maple trees and an expanse of gray sky. The sun was already starting to set as the days got shorter. To think he might not have seen another one.

She turned her head and reached for his hand. She interlocked her fingers in his. "You should have called me at work. I could have dropped whatever I was doing. When you weren't home, I didn't know what to think."

"So you missed me?" he asked.

She nodded. "It's true."

He pulled her hand to his chest, and she lay down next to him. She sniffed. "You know, I wasn't planning on getting attached to you. You represented everything that I didn't want right now. Male companionship. Help. A loss of independence. And…well…I guess that pretty much covers it. I was convinced I was in my 'solo' phase of life."

"And now?"

"Now when I realize I could have lost you, that doesn't sound so appealing."

He smiled. "I take this to mean I can still count on your homemade cookies for a while?"

She smacked him gently on the shoulder.

"Hey! I'm the injured party here!"

"Not your shoulder." She rubbed it anyway.

"Well, Fred will be delighted to hear that you're staying on. He has abandonment issues, you know."

"I have no doubt he'd track me down and sit on me until I came back."

All of a sudden the baby kicked.

Hunt looked down. Lying next to her, he felt it, too. "The baby?"

She chuckled. "Wants to be part of the act."

Hunt held his hand above her belly. "It's okay?" He placed his fingers lightly on her shirt.

"You can press harder," she said. "There, did you feel that? That was some kick."

"Incredible," he marveled, shaking his head.

Sarah smiled. She loved feeling the baby move, and she had thought that it was the best sensation she had ever experienced. Until Hunt got to experience it along with her. She could feel the tears welling instantaneously.

"Hey, what's wrong?" Hunt said, worried. "I don't want you getting upset. Not with the problems you've already got."

Sarah sniffed away the tears. "Don't be ridiculous. It's just the hormones. Besides, can't a girl have tears of happiness?"

"Well, as long as it's happiness. We can't take any more excitement in our little temporary family for now."

"I guess we are a kind of family in a weird way."

"I guess we're both a little weird, although I'm not sure how Fred would take it."

She sniffed again, the contentment reaching its way down to her toes. "Enough. You can't be all that bad if you can make jokes." She stretched to get the bag she'd put on the end of the bed. "Look, I packed you some toiletries, another T-shirt and boxers, and a pair of jeans. Oh, and socks. There's a bathrobe, too, but I couldn't find any slippers. I also found a recent issue of the *New Yorker*. I'll bring some books tomorrow morning if you think it will be a few days."

"Thanks. I'm not sure how long they're going to keep me."

"So do I need to make some kind of arrangement to get your car out of the hospital garage?"

Hunt lifted his hand from her stomach and rubbed her forearm. "Actually, I didn't drive here. I got a lift."

"Rufus? Katarina said you had called him?"

"I did call him, but he had his appointment with you, and I didn't want to make him late." He paused. "Don't be mad."

"Why would I be mad, other than the fact that you were being noble and refused to bother me?"

"That's not what I meant. I'm trying to explain that it seemed like everyone I knew wasn't available. I was desperate. So I called the last person on my list."

Sarah raised her eyebrows and waited.

Hunt opened his mouth. "Zach."

She thought a moment, then stretched and kissed him gently on the forehead. "I'm glad he was there for you." She squeezed his hand and snuggled more closely. "Now I've got a confession to make."

He raised his eyebrows. "Is it dirty?"

She rolled her eyes. "I'll blame that on the drugs. No, it's not dirty. I needed a ride here tonight, too, and I was running out of options. So, I went to the bottom of the list."

"You called—"

"Your mother," she said.

"I can't believe it. She isn't here, though, is she?" Hunt balanced himself up on his elbow.

"She's waiting outside the room, in the hallway." Sarah pointed toward the door. She could feel his body stiffen. "Hunt, she was really worried. I can vouch for it—her hands were shaking on the wheel of the car."

Hunt gave her a skeptical look. "She was probably concerned that people might assume that she was sick— she couldn't handle that."

"Hunt, now that you know you're in no danger, why not be generous? Frankly, if I can call my mother for advice, you can see yours now."

He harrumphed. "All right. On one condition."

She eyed him dubiously. "Am I going to like this?"

"You tell me." He raised both hands to either side of her face and kissed her—affirming lust, relief and life.

CHAPTER TWENTY-FOUR

HUNT WATCHED THE SLOW DRIP of the antibiotics with growing impatience. A full course took one hour, one more hour of his life that he was forced to stay in the hospital. After three nights he'd had enough. He'd finished the newest John Grisham, the latest issue of *The Economist,* and a book on birthing with pictures that Hunt would sooner forget. His mother had even come to visit—twice more. It was awkward, but Hunt had to admit she was trying. Now, he was ready to leave.

His doctors had decided that because he had been fever-free for forty-eight hours and the swelling had substantially subsided, *and* the CT scan showing his lymph nodes were clear, he could head home. He'd have to take oral antibiotics, and he had instructions to take it easy and schedule a follow-up appointment in a week.

Sure! Whatever! Hunt had already packed his few belongings hours ago. He was more than ready to have the PICC line removed from his arm. And if they didn't take it out soon, he was going to scream.

Sarah had counseled patience. This morning when she'd stopped by on her way to work, she had said to call when he was ready, no matter what time. Katarina would drive her now that they had come back from their jaunt up north.

Hunt stared at the drip. This was not happening soon enough.

"Knock, knock. Can I come in, or is this a bad moment?" Ben stood by the corner of the curtain dividing the room in two.

Hunt waved him in. "It's a bad moment only because I'm still here. Come and amuse me in my misery. Just move my stuff off the chair." He pointed to the armchair by the window.

Ben lowered the bursting shopping bag to the floor and settled into the chair. It hadn't exactly been built for someone his size, and he shifted back and forth. He managed to get semicomfortable and crossed his legs at his ankles. "So, I hear they're letting you out today."

"And none too soon. I'm feeling one hundred percent better."

Ben tilted his head to get a better look. "Still a bit puffy there." He held up his hand to his own cheek to show what he meant.

"You should have seen me a few days ago. Really strange. Talk about *Night of the Living Dead*. Anyway, that's all in the past."

"Glad to hear it."

There was an awkward silence while Ben drummed his fingers on the arm of the chair.

"How was the trip?" Hunt asked finally.

Ben held up his hand. "The trip was good. It was the first time we'd all gone away together as a family. One of those bonding experiences. Only now Katarina feels so close to Matt, she's already talking about 'empty nest syndrome' when he goes away to college."

"But that's…that's still more than a year away, right?"

"Right. But you know women."

"Actually, not really."

"Neither do I, really," Ben agreed.

They both sniffed.

"So, Sarah will be there still when you go home?" Ben asked a little too casually.

"Yeah. She already tells me she's been baking up a storm in anticipation of my arrival. And Wanda stepped in to help with Fred. She's more or less adopted him when nobody's home, taking him for walks, feeding him far too many treats. Sarah told me that her own dog died recently, so I think Fred is good therapy."

Hunt shook his head. "That Fred. Sarah tells me he misses me so much that he won't leave my bed, so to keep him company, she's sleeping there, too."

Ben nodded, his mouth open. "You don't say? Anything else you want to tell me about Fred or…ah… Sarah?"

Hunt cleared his throat. "Not really, but listen, Ben. I want to talk to you about the business."

Ben waited.

Hunt wiped his mouth. "You know how you've been after me to get back to work? Well, now that I had time to think, especially the last few days, I've come to some conclusions."

Ben cocked his head. "I'm all ears."

"Let me just come out and say it then. I'm ready to go back to work, but I don't want to go back to work with you."

Ben uncrossed his legs and sat forward. "I'm a problem?"

"No, it's not you. You're a great friend, and I couldn't ask for a better business partner. No, it's more that I've decided to retire from the world of high finance. I've had a lot of fun working with you, solving problems, getting results, but it's not what I want to do right now, not what I have a passion for. One thing I've learned, life can be short—very short. And there's no point in doing what you don't love."

"And have you decided what you want to do next?"

"Don't laugh. I was thinking of going to medical school. I know I'm already thirty-five, and I won't be able to practice until I'm in my forties, but I figure if I have to have a midlife crisis, it's about as good as any. I talked it over with Sarah already, and she thinks it's a natural fit, considering what I'd been through. Tell me. Am I being crazy?"

"I've heard stranger. Actually, this trip with the family got me thinking, too."

Hunt leaned forward, hanging onto the IV stand. "Oh, yeah? Please, don't tell me you want to run a B and B?"

"No way. Those places are scary. No, just hear me out—there's a whole thought process going on." He held up his hand.

Hunt nodded.

"Anyway, I kept thinking more and more about how great it was to be together as a family, and then Lena had us all over for dinner last night. There she was, going on and on about how she'd read this magazine at PT and that got her thinking about how she'd never gone to Montana, and how maybe she could learn fly-fishing."

"Sure, why not. She's perfectly healthy enough to travel," Hunt agreed.

Ben held up his hand. "Just wait—hear me out. Anyhow, I told her I'd be happy to teach her, even fly out with her, make it a family event with Matt and Katarina in fact. After all, Matt hasn't been back to Colorado since he came east. We could combine the two trips into one."

"Am I allowed to say that sounds great?"

"Yeah, that's what I thought. A kind of a father-son experience with the grandmother and stepmom thing thrown in for good measure. Then when we got home, I got to thinking that it would be a great experience for other people, as well. I could act as a guide for other families, a multiple generation thing. I could even start by teaching a course on fly-fishing at the Adult School for parents and children, grandparents and grandkids— kind of a warm-up for the trip. Then for people who couldn't afford the travel, I could even start some kind of foundation, promoting intergenerational travel as a way to foster stable upbringings. Heck, I have more than enough money to get the thing off the ground, then maybe get some donations to help out."

"Somehow I feel you're touching me up for a dona- tion, am I right?" Hunt laughed. "I'd be happy to. But I have to say, you must be having a midlife crisis when you start mentioning the Adult School."

"Kind of scary, isn't it?" Ben nodded. "But, you know, I think it probably is a good time to wind the investment firm down. I've got enough going on helping out with Katarina's business on the side, plus when the baby comes…"

Hunt nearly yanked the IV out of his arm. "When the baby comes? Katarina's pregnant?"

Ben beamed. "Yup. The whole trip, she was feel- ing a little under the weather, and then we put two and two together and made a midnight run to an all-night CVS. We weren't really trying—but then we weren't not trying either, mind you. Anyway, she took the test and bingo!"

Hunt whistled. "Congrats, old buddy. So no hard feelings about dissolving our partnership?"

Ben shook his head. "A little bit of sadness maybe. We had a good run. But it seems that we're both ready to open a new chapter in our lives."

FRED BOUNDED ON THE BED and landed directly on Hunt. Hunt swore and rolled over. "I missed you, too. How was class?" Hunt asked, rubbing the dog's ears.

"Class was grueling. We learned loose-leash walking and 'sit,'" Sarah said. She stood by the open door to his bedroom. "But as much as I love Wanda, I'm not going with her again. She's just too competitive. We almost came to blows with Toulouse."

She waddled into the room and sat down on the edge of the bed. Unconsciously, she was drawn to cuddling the dog, too. "So, enough of this lollygagging in bed, Hunt Phox. I let you sleep like a baby for two days after coming home from the hospital, but now it's Sunday. I think it's time for a change of scenery—especially if you're going to be ready for obedience class next week."

"Can I hold off on the loose-leash walking? 'Sit' I think I'm up for." He abandoned Fred's ears for Sarah's arm and pulled her down to offer a kiss.

She pulled back and laughed. "All right. But just this once. I don't want it getting out that I'm getting soft in my old age."

"But I like you any which way—soft, hard." He

tugged her harder and she fell next to him. "Here on the bed's good, too."

"I take it you're not talking about sleeping."

"Do I look like I'm talking about sleeping?"

The sheet covered Hunt to his waist, and even with a pair of boxers on, Sarah caught his drift. "Are you sure you're up for this?" She groaned and covered her face. "Sorry, I didn't mean that."

"You can't begin to understand just how happy I am to say that, yes, indeed, I am." Hunt grinned broadly and turned on his side to face her. He brought his hand to the zipper of her hoodie. "Hey, this is mine, isn't it?" he asked.

"You don't mind, do you? I'm getting a little short of things to wear that still fit me."

"You can wear or not wear anything of mine you want." He unzipped the sweatshirt. "You want this, don't you?" He looked up.

She nodded and smiled. "I can't think of anything I want more. Only I have a favor to ask."

He raised his eyebrows. Fred pricked up his ears.

"I want the curtains to stay closed and the lights turned off. My stretch marks are just disgusting."

"Like I haven't seen them at the pool?"

"This is different. We're not bouncing up and down in front of a bunch of pregnant women and old folks."

"I should hope not. But I don't know why you are so worried about the way you look. I'm the one who can count every rib. Not exactly the height of machismo."

"Excuse me, after all the cookies I've made not every rib is visible. I bet your pants can stay up on your hips now without the benefit of a belt." Sarah looked down.

In the course of discussing their individual body

faults, he had managed to get off not only her hoodie but her bra, and she was naked from the waist up.

Hunt shooed the dog off the bed and discarded his boxers to the floor. He twisted to slip down her warm-up pants and underpants at the same time. "Now that we've dismissed this whole light or no light objection of yours, could you lift your hip up and help me?"

"Who said I'd given up?" Nevertheless, she raised her hips, and helped him by kicking off her clothes with her feet.

He held up the sheet and let her slip beneath.

Sarah snuggled up against him, face-to-face, her naked body against his. She ran her toes down his lower legs.

"Hey, give me your lips," he said.

"Why?" She did as he asked.

And he took her head in his hands and kissed her with a fierceness that took her breath away. Then he tucked a lock of her hair behind her ear and kissed her sweetly on the tip of her nose. "I got to warn you," he said.

"You need more time?" she asked, pulling back.

"No, just the opposite. I wanted to say, that while I enjoy all this kissing and cuddling—and which I will gladly resume at another time—I'm not sure I can wait too much longer."

Sarah could have screamed with joy. "Good, because I can't wait even that long."

She got to her knees, and with less than balletic grace straddled his hips, positioned herself above his arousal and plunged down, enveloping him in her warmth.

Their coupling was swift and intense, a mating in every sense. And when they climaxed at the same time, it was an agonizing release, and the only way to come down was with silence. With a tender pat here and a gentle rub there.

And when Fred ventured into the bedroom five minutes later, they were asleep in each other's arms, leaving room for the dog to curl up at the end, nestled against their entwined feet.

BY THE TIME THEY WOKE, it was dark. Sarah rotated her head to the side and lifted her neck to look at the bedside clock. "Gee, it's already seven."

Fred rose and stretched. He delicately inched his way up the bed and plopped down, his nose between Hunt's and Sarah's. He licked them both.

Sarah wiped her nose. "I guess he's trying to tell us he wants his dinner."

Hunt wiggled his hips closer to hers and wrapped his arm around her shoulders. "Well, he can wait a few minutes. I want to enjoy you more." He rubbed his cheek against hers and kissed the side of her head. He breathed in deeply. "I want to remember this moment."

Sarah closed her eyes and smiled. "Me, too. You know, I don't want this to go to your head, but you're pretty special."

She felt him smile against her hair.

"And why shouldn't I let it go to my head?" he asked mischievously.

"Because then you'll be even more insufferable than you already are, and then it would simply take too much effort to keep knocking you down to size."

He slipped his arm out from underneath her and propped himself up on an elbow. "Are you threatening to leave me?"

Sarah looked at him and blinked. She realized he was

being serious. "No," she said. And *she* realized she was being serious. Because she loved him.

She reached for his hand. "All my life I tried to be everything to everybody else—and failed miserably at it."

"But—"

She put her hands to his lips. His beautiful, sexy lips. "When I was growing up, I tried to be the type of daughter I thought my parents wanted—someone who never wanted to leave home and wanted to study animal husbandry and make my own curtains."

"I don't need curtains."

"Quiet! I mean it!" she warned him. Fred hunkered down immediately.

"Anyway, I soon knew I wasn't cut out to be a farmer's wife. That's when I thought I found the man of my dreams and followed him to New York to be the dutiful indie music groupie. Well, he didn't make much music, and anyway, I found it boring hanging out in clubs. Then came the young professional scene in Manhattan, the hip student, the committed professional and then the incredibly competent mom-to-be. And all this time I was trying to fulfill a role that I thought everyone expected me to fulfill. Only I've finally come to understand that none of them were me."

"They weren't?" he asked.

She inhaled deeply. "No. Because what I've come to realize through you—yes, you—is that what I really should have been doing all along is to be true to myself. Because only that way would I find real happiness."

"So have you found yourself?" Hunt asked.

Sarah nodded. "I think so. No, I know so." She looked him in the eyes. "I've found what I was looking for. A home. And a family. Because home is that special place in my heart, wherever I have my family—the baby, you, even Fred."

At the sound of his name, Fred tentatively stood up and dipped his head to hers.

"I love you," she said.

"You love Fred?" Hunt asked.

"Not Fred. Well…yes…I love Fred. But what I really mean, is I love you." Sarah looked at Hunt. "So? Aren't you going to say anything?"

Hunt frowned. "I'm still thinking about you being an indie band groupie."

Sarah frowned.

He kissed her hand. "You know what's so great about you, Sarah Halverson?—you're focused on what's essential. And you make *me* focus on what's essential. So, as much as I would like to fall back on my usual witty repartee, and make light of your declaration, I won't."

"You won't?"

"No, because it deserves equal honesty." He swallowed. Then inhaled slowly. "Just practicing a little Lamaze therapy."

Sarah had venom in her eyes.

"Sorry, sorry. Just because I'm having problems altering the habits of a lifetime, doesn't mean I don't love you."

"Wait a minute. Could you say that without all the double negatives?"

"I." He kissed one eye. "Love." He kissed the other. "You." He kissed the tip of her upturned nose. Then drew back to drink in her expression. "Very, very, much." And then he kissed her lips tenderly.

Fred nudged between them.

"Oh, all right." Hunt threw up his hands. "I'll get up and get you your dinner." He swung his legs over the side of the bed. "See now. You've got him being a slave driver, too."

"I'll get his food," Sarah offered, pushing herself to a sitting position.

Hunt bent over and retrieved his boxers and reached for a pair of sweatpants. "No!" He held out his hand. "For once, you don't get to do anything for anyone else. You get to be a lady of leisure."

Sarah lay back in bed and sighed. "I think I like the sound of that. Hurry back, though."

Hunt slipped one leg in the pants and hopped over to her side. "Quickly, my love, as soon as I feed and walk our demented dog."

She laughed.

He stole a kiss while she was still laughing. It felt fizzy.

He leaned over the bed and looked at her. "All kidding aside—"

"All kidding aside…"

"I want this to last longer than the baby's birth," he said.

She nodded. "Me, too."

"So you'll move in?"

"But what about my place?"

"Details. We'll work it out."

"Well, in that case, okay. I'll move in." She could feel the happiness welling inside.

He looked away and then back. "I've got to warn you, though. I can't think long-term yet."

"If you're talking about dying, don't. I mean, I could

be hit by a bus tomorrow. There're some things you just can't know. There *are* no guarantees."

"But I've had cancer."

"That's in the past. And the statistics are now over-whelmingly in your favor."

Hunt nodded. "Logically, I know you're right, but emotionally, I'm not there yet. I can't make any promises."

"Was I asking for promises?"

He shook his head and grabbed her hand. "You're too good for me."

"I know." She smiled. And with time, she knew he'd truly realize the prize they had found, truly realize that what they had together would last a lifetime.

CHAPTER TWENTY-FIVE

Three weeks later...

"LIKE THE LOOK, HON," Hunt said, rising from the chair in Sarah's waiting room. He closed the review book for the med-school admissions test that he had started plowing through a couple of weeks ago.

He had been a chemical engineering major, and he'd actually fulfilled the course requirements for med school. And as he somewhat sheepishly admitted to Sarah since it was damaging evidence for a self-proclaimed lazy-bones, his three-point-eight grade point average, wasn't too shabby either. Still, cracking the books in his thirties was tougher than he had expected.

"But it's not like having a baby," Sarah was wont to reply when he moaned particularly loudly.

He wasn't moaning now. Well, maybe internally, and for different reasons. The love of his life, now a week away from her due date and in all her voluptuous glory, had just appeared in the reception room of her office dressed as a very pregnant French maid. *I love Halloween,* he thought.

Rosemary finished shutting down her computer and got up to empty the coffeepot. "I'll see you two love-birds tomorrow then," she said, slipping on a ski jacket and adjusting the reindeer antlers in her hair. It was an office tradition to dress up for Halloween. "And I can't thank you enough, Hunt, for running to Kmart for me to get candy on sale. I never would have had the chance before the hordes start descending."

Sarah came over. "I recognize what you're doing, you know." She twirled her finger at him threateningly. "You're attempting to turn the office staff's loyalty to you—picking up everybody's dry cleaning, coming in and acting all charming. And just to show you that it's working…"

She kissed him on the lips. Then she stepped back to study Hunt's costume. "I could get used to the look," she said.

He was dressed like a swashbuckling pirate, with a black eye patch and a rakishly angled red bandana over his hair, which had grown longer over the weeks. Sarah liked the long, loose curls so much she'd refused to let him get them cut. She also liked the white shirt unbuttoned to the waistband of his tight black pants, which she vaguely recognized as a pair she'd used for yoga. Not that she'd ever fit into them again.

"Shall we?" He removed the shawl she had over her arm and draped it over her shoulders. He picked up his review book. "See you tomorrow, Rosemary. We're off to torture ourselves at water aerobics." He didn't bother to hide the sarcasm.

"Don't listen to him, Rosemary. He loves it, and it's made a big difference already."

"I think all the walking and jogging and the weight program you've got me on has contributed some, too."

Sarah waved goodbye and headed for the car. They'd switched to her Honda Accord from his Porsche since the bucket seats were just too unmanageable at this point.

After she buckled up, she turned to Hunt, not waiting for him to pull out of the parking lot. "I've been thinking."

"Hmm. Always dangerous." He turned into the road.

"I know we just finished redoing the little bedroom for a nursery, but what about doing something with the bedroom downstairs? I mean, now that I've rented out my place, I've got some extra money, and seeing as Wanda is committed to taking care of the baby and Fred…"

Hunt came to a stoplight and looked askance. "Sarah, we've been through this before. You're to save that money, and Ben or I or even Katarina will be glad to help you invest it. But even without worrying about the money, I think it's time to hold off on any more renovations. Wanda's going to move in with Lena anyway, and that's right around the block."

The light changed, and he turned left to get to the middle school.

"Okay, we can hold off on that room, but don't you think you should really look into retiling the lap pool on the roof? Even you said it needs doing."

"Let's wait. With the baby coming, there might be other priorities to consider." He hadn't told her that he'd already made provisions to shift some of his investments to a college savings account. He figured that would be a good gift to announce after their baby was born.

It was true. Somewhere in the past few weeks he had shifted from thinking of the baby as "her" baby to "their" baby. Of course Zach would be as much a part of the baby's life as he wanted, but Hunt couldn't help feeling what Ben had called an "emotional bond."

Hunt parked the car, and Sarah was already getting out while he reached in the backseat to get their gym bags.

"Here you are." He passed a bag to Sarah. "I'll see you in there after I change."

"I just hope this bikini still stays in place. I can't believe how big I've gotten in the last couple of weeks."

"It might liven things up a bit if it didn't. On the other hand, just think how Doris would blow her whistle in all the excitement!" Hunt chuckled at the thought of their instructor losing her cool. He gave her a peck on the cheek and they separated at the entrances to the men's and women's locker rooms.

Two minutes later, Hunt had just managed to change his tight pirate pants for his swim trunks when Wanda burst into the men's locker room.

"Huntington, come quickly. Sarah needs you."

Hunt's heart leaped in his chest. With his unbuttoned shirt ballooning to the sides, he rushed into the women's locker room. "Where is she?" he asked, racing past several women from the class in various states of undress. "Don't worry," he called out, waving to them as he moved quickly past.

There were screeches and shouts of, "A man! You shouldn't be in here!"

"I'm going to be a doctor, so it means nothing," he said on the run.

Wanda pointed to the last row of lockers. "She's back there, halfway down the aisle."

Hunt sped on. He rounded the corner and came to a screeching halt. Sarah was standing with her legs pressed close together and an agonized look on her face. The low-cut blouse to her costume was unbuttoned. Her breasts billowed out. She looked up. "My water broke." She sounded in shock.

Lena grabbed her towel. "Don't worry, we can dry you up. Here." She wrapped it around Sarah's waist and patted her dry.

"This is great!" Hunt put his arm around her shoulders. "That means the baby's coming. And don't worry about the mess. We're driving your car, don't you remember?"

Sarah narrowed her eyes. "Please remind me why I put up with you."

Hunt took her hand and squeezed it. His own was shaking like a leaf. After a moment, the drills of the Lamaze class clicked in. "I've got to call Julie and Katarina."

Wanda had her cell phone in her hand. "I'm already on top of that. As the designated alternative grandmother, I know my role." She had announced to Sarah and Hunt the other day that that was her title, and hers alone.

"What's going on? Somebody said a strange man with one eye came barging into the women's locker room!" It was Carl, the elderly man with the vertical bi-pass scar on his chest who was also taking the class. He brandished a flipper.

Hunt shifted his black eye patch to the top of his bandanna. "It's just me, Carl."

A high-pitched whistle pierced the air. All heads turned.

Doris stood at the end of the aisle, brandishing her whistle. "What seems to be the problem here?"

"Hold your horses, Doris," Wanda snapped. "It's Sarah. She's going to have her baby."

Doris stood up straight. "Quick then, a plan of action."

"Anything." Carl stepped forward.

Lena pulled on a cardigan over her swimsuit. "Hunt will take Sarah to the hospital. But, Carl, why don't you retrieve Hunt's things from the men's room and meet him by their car outside?"

Carl rushed out with purpose.

"I'll get Sarah's things and come with Sarah and Hunt. I'll also call Rufus to take care of the dog," Lena said.

Sarah glanced up, looking confused at all the commotion around her. "And could you call Zach's and Hunt's moms? They should know, too."

"I've already got them in my phone," Wanda said.

"What about my suitcase and pillow?" Sarah asked.

"Don't worry. I'll stop by the house and get them," Wanda reassured.

"They're in the bedroom." Hunt managed to button up Sarah's blouse out of order but good enough. He grabbed her shawl from the bench and wrapped it around her shoulders. "We're good to go then?"

She nodded, holding the towel around her waist. "As good as I'll ever be." She glanced over at Doris. "I guess this means we'll miss the last class."

"Then I'll just have to hold you two to a makeup session. I always expect full participation and completion of assignments."

Hunt pushed open the locker door with his shoulder, and he held Sarah, guiding her down the stairs to the car. "You know you're going to have to marry me," he said before they had even gotten outside.

"Why, because the baby needs a father?"

"No, I think the baby has more than enough fathers. Enough grandmothers and aunts *and* uncles. But I think it's time before he—"

"Or she…"

"Or she has any sisters or brothers that there's at least a designated official wife and a designated official husband."

Sarah stopped and studied his face. Besides the wry smile, she saw something more—much more. She saw his love and commitment. She saw the possibility of a future, a future together. Her heart raced. "I love you, you know."

"I know," he said, his voice full of wonder. "And I love you."

Lena glanced at one and then the other and offered a sigh of contentment. "Matt will be so pleased that I made him practice the Mendelssohn." Then she quickly regrouped. "Excuse me, we all have our jobs to perform." Lena shooed them down the path toward the car. Carl was waiting with Hunt's clothes.

Hunt had his eyes elsewhere. "So this means you accept, right?" he asked Sarah. For once, he didn't sound all that confident.

Sarah shrugged coyly. "I suppose it would provide Fred with some much needed stability."

"Ouch! Now I know what it feels like when I kid you!" Hunt turned to Carl. "Do you think it's improper to punch a lady in the arm even under extreme circumstances? She does it to me all the time."

"Well…I'm old-school and—"

Lena threw up her hands. "Forget the punches! Forget the schools! We have bigger fish to fry." Lena grabbed the clothes from Carl. She found the car keys and thrust them at Hunt. "Here, be a man and drive."

"Hold on." Sarah grabbed Hunt with both hands. She was in a hurry to get to the hospital, but she needed to clear up something first. "So does this mean you've gotten over your fear of dying tomorrow or the next day or the next?"

"If you can go through giving birth, then I think the least I can do is to live a long life. Besides, I can already visualize us having wheelchair races down Main Street. So I'm warning you—better stay in shape. I can be very competitive."

Sarah beamed. "No matter. I'm the one who's already won." She bent down gingerly to get in the passenger seat. "And by the way. The answer's yes."

* * * * *

COMING NEXT MONTH

Available January 11, 2011

#1680 A LITTLE TEXAS
Hometown U.S.A.
Liz Talley

#1681 HER GREAT EXPECTATIONS
Summerside Stories
Joan Kilby

#1682 HERE COMES THE GROOM
Going Back
Karina Bliss

#1683 HOME TO HARMONY
Dawn Atkins

#1684 BECAUSE OF JANE
Lenora Worth

#1685 NANNY NEXT DOOR
Single Father
Michelle Celmer

REQUEST YOUR FREE BOOKS!

2 FREE NOVELS PLUS 2 FREE GIFTS!

HARLEQUIN®

Super Romance®

Exciting, emotional, unexpected!

YES! Please send me 2 FREE Harlequin® Superromance® novels and my 2 FREE gifts (gifts are worth about $10). After receiving them, if I don't wish to receive any more books, I can return the shipping statement marked "cancel." If I don't cancel, I will receive 6 brand-new novels every month and be billed just $4.69 per book in the U.S. or $5.24 per book in Canada. That's a saving of at least 15% off the cover price! It's quite a bargain! Shipping and handling is just 50¢ per book.* I understand that accepting the 2 free books and gifts places me under no obligation to buy anything. I can always return a shipment and cancel at any time. Even if I never buy another book from Harlequin, the two free books and gifts are mine to keep forever.

135/336 HDN E5P4

Name _____ (PLEASE PRINT)

Address _____ Apt. #

City _____ State/Prov. _____ Zip/Postal Code

Signature (if under 18, a parent or guardian must sign)

Mail to the **Harlequin Reader Service:**
IN U.S.A.: P.O. Box 1867, Buffalo, NY 14240-1867
IN CANADA: P.O. Box 609, Fort Erie, Ontario L2A 5X3

Not valid for current subscribers to Harlequin Superromance books.
**Are you a current subscriber to Harlequin Superromance books
and want to receive the larger-print edition?
Call 1-800-873-8635 today!**

* Terms and prices subject to change without notice. Prices do not include applicable taxes. N.Y. residents add applicable sales tax. Canadian residents will be charged applicable provincial taxes and GST. Offer not valid in Quebec. This offer is limited to one order per household. All orders subject to approval. Credit or debit balances in a customer's account(s) may be offset by any other outstanding balance owed by or to the customer. Please allow 4 to 6 weeks for delivery. Offer available while quantities last.

Your Privacy: Harlequin Books is committed to protecting your privacy. Our Privacy Policy is available online at www.eHarlequin.com or upon request from the Reader Service. From time to time we make our lists of customers available to reputable third parties who may have a product or service of interest to you. If you would prefer we not share your name and address, please check here. ☐

Help us get it right—We strive for accurate, respectful and relevant communications. To clarify or modify your communication preferences, visit us at www.ReaderService.com/consumerschoice.

HSR10R

HARLEQUIN®

A Romance

FOR EVERY MOOD™

Spotlight on

Classic

Quintessential, modern love stories
that are romance at its finest.

See the next page
to enjoy a sneak peek from
the Harlequin Presents® series.

*Harlequin Presents® is thrilled
to introduce the first installment of
an epic tale of passion and drama by*
**USA TODAY *Bestselling Author
Penny Jordan*!**

*When buttoned-up Giselle first meets
the devastatingly handsome Saul Parenti,
the heat between them is explosive....*

"LET ME GET THIS STRAIGHT. Are you actually suggesting that I would stoop to that kind of game playing?"

Saul came out from behind his desk and walked toward her. Giselle could smell his hot male scent and it was making her dizzy, igniting a low, dull, pulsing ache that was taking over her whole body.

Giselle defended her suspicions. "You don't want me here."

"No," Saul agreed, "I don't."

And then he did what he had sworn he would not do, cursing himself beneath his breath as he reached for her, pulling her fiercely into his arms and kissing her with all the pent-up fury she had aroused in him from the moment he had first seen her.

Giselle certainly *wanted* to resist him. But the hand she raised to push him away developed a will of its own and was sliding along his bare arm beneath the sleeve of his shirt, and the body that should have been arching away from him was instead melting into him.

Beneath the pressure of his kiss he could feel and taste her gasp of undeniable response to him. He wanted to devour her, take her and drive them both until they were equally satiated—even whilst the anger within him that she should make him feel that way roared and burned its resentment of his need.

She was helpless, Giselle recognized, totally unable to withstand the storm lashing at her, able only to cling to the man who was the cause of it and pray that she would survive.

Somewhere else in the building a door banged. The sound exploded into the sensual tension that had enclosed them, driving them apart. Saul's chest was rising and falling as he fought for control; Giselle's whole body was trembling.

Without a word she turned and ran.

Find out what happens when Saul and Giselle succumb to their irresistible desire in

THE RELUCTANT SURRENDER

Available January 2011 from Harlequin Presents®

MARGARET WAY

Wealthy Australian,
Secret Son

Rohan was Charlotte's shining white knight
until he disappeared—before she had
the chance to tell him she was pregnant.

But when Rohan returns years later as
a self-made millionaire, could the blond,
blue-eyed little boy and Charlotte's heart
keep him from leaving again?

Available January 2011

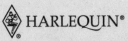

C.C. COBURN
Colorado Cowboy

American Romance's
Men of the West

It had been fifteen years since Luke O'Malley,
divorced father of three, last saw his high school
sweetheart, Megan Montgomery. Luke is shocked to
discover they have a son, Cody, a rebellious teen on his
way to juvenile detention. The last thing either of them
expected was nuptials. Will these strangers rekindle
their love or is the past too far behind them?

Available January
wherever books are sold.

"LOVE, HOME & HAPPINESS"